THE DEAD MAN'S STOLEN BOOK

A MOLLY GREY COZY MYSTERY

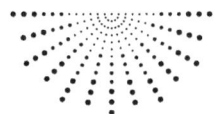

DONNA DOYLE

© 2019 PUREREAD LTD

PUREREAD.COM

CONTENTS

INTRODUCTION

A PERSONAL WORD FROM PUREREAD

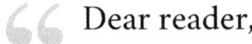 Dear reader,

Do you love a good mystery? So do we! Nothing is more pleasing than a page turner that keeps you guessing until the very last page.

In our Christian cozy mysteries you can be certain that there won't be any gruesome or gory scenes, swearing or anything else upsetting, just good clean fun as you unravel the mystery together with our marvelous characters.

Thank you for choosing PureRead!

To find out more about PureRead mysteries and receive new release information and other goodies from Donna Doyle go to our website PureRead.com/donnadoyle

* * *

Enjoy The Story!

BE TRUE TO THYSELF...

Thou must be true thyself
If thou the truth would teach
The soul must overflow if thou
Another's soul would reach
It needs the overflow of heart
To give the lips full speech

Think truly, and thy thoughts
Shall the world's famine feed;
Speak truly, and each word of thine
Shall be a fruitful seed;
Live truly, and thy life shall be
A great and noble creed.

H.Bonar

CHAPTER ONE

"I've got something to tell you, Julian…"

The old man whispered in a hoarse voice which was barely audible, but he squeezed Papa Julian's hands, and motioned with his wide, green eyes that he had something of great importance to tell.

"What is it, Preston?" Papa Julian leaned over until his ear almost touched the lips of the dying man.

"The pain is passing," Preston whispered, while his breath came in ragged, shallow gasps. "I hear voices…"

"Voices?" Papa Julian asked as he listened intently to what the man was whispering. He did not hear anything besides the clicking of the wall clock and the labored breathing of his friend. Of course he didn't. Dying people always experienced things that they, the living, could not detect. He stared for a moment at Miss Molly Gertrude who sat at the opposite side of the bed. Her eyes were closed, but her lips were moving as she was saying a prayer.

"What kind of voices do you hear, Preston?"

A weak smile appeared around the thin lips in his gaunt face, but his eyes still held a sparkling little light. "The angels are coming… the road has come to an end."

"I know," Papa Julian whispered and he had to swallow hard. His friend, his mentor, the one who had always helped him in his career as a pastor of Calmhaven Trinity Church, was dying. Soon Preston Linney would be no more, and although Papa Julian was happy because the struggle for Preston was over, a deep sense of sorrow filled his heart. He had no doubts as to the destination of his good friend, and he knew that the voices Preston was hearing were no hallucination or some quirk of the brain in the moment of death, but that angels were indeed filling the room in order to accompany Preston to his eternal home. But he would miss the wise and godly counsel of this man who had had such an impact on his life. Life

2

without Preston Linney would just not be quite the same.

"Julian..." Preston whispered again. "Look in the... dr... drawer." The poor man could hardly get out the words. Papa Julian pressed his lips into a fine line and looked around. Where was a drawer?

And indeed, at the opposite end of the bed stood a small nut wood cupboard. Its top held several framed pictures. There was a good-sized picture of Preston with a child on a swing and a smaller one with a woman who had a gigantic smile that was holding up a kitten. "You want to see the pictures?" Papa Julian asked.

Preston shook his head, accompanied by a small frown. "D-Drawer."

Molly Gertrude had opened her eyes and stared at Papa Julian with questioning eyes. Papa Julian motioned at the cabinet with his head. "Would you look in the drawer, dear? There's something in there that Preston wants."

The old woman nodded, and got up with some difficulty while leaning on her cane.

As a faithful member of Calmhaven Trinity church, and a close friend of Papa Julian she often visited the pastor in his study, but that morning she had not come on a social visit, but wanted to discuss business. She and her cheerful helper Dora Brightside were in charge of the Cozy Bridal Agency, Calmhaven's only wedding agency, and she and Papa Julian needed to discuss the details of an upcoming wedding event. But things rarely turn out exactly as expected. No sooner had Molly Gertrude entered the pastor's study, than the news had reached them that Preston Linney had not long to live.

"Come with me, Molly Gertrude," the pastor had asked. "I need your support as much as Preston needs mine." Thus, Molly Gertrude had come along and she shuffled to the drawers.

"What am I looking for?" Molly Gertrude asked when she stood in front of the cabinet.

Preston Linney whispered something to Papa Julian.

"Top drawer," Papa Julian reported back. "There is a book."

Molly Gertrude pulled on the knobs and the drawer slid open. Papa Julian followed her with his eyes, and even Preston Linney was trying to lift his head so he could have a better view.

Molly Gertrude rummaged around a bit and then exclaimed, "Ah… this must be it." She turned around and held up an old looking book. It was bound in brown leather, but cracked and dry with age, and the stitching was barely holding it together. Molly Gertrude sneezed. No wonder, as the thing smelled musty and old.

"Is this what you need?" Molly Gertrude asked.

Papa Julian nodded, and Molly Gertrude shuffled back to the bed and handed it to the pastor. Preston Linney fell back on his pillow, but his face held a relieved expression. He motioned with his hand for Papa Julian to lean closer again so he could offer an explanation.

"What is it Preston?" Papa Julian asked.

"R-Read the title," Preston mumbled.

Papa Julian stared at the book, and as he read the title a shock curled up through his spine.

Pilgrim's Progress
By John Bunyan

Papa Julian blinked his eyes and leaned closer to Preston Linney. "Is-is this an old copy of the beloved book of John Bunyan?" he asked.

Preston shook his head. "Not copy...First edition."

The first edition of the Pilgrim's Progress? How was such a thing even possible?

"How did you get this?" Papa Julian asked, way louder than he had wanted to. For a moment he almost forgot he was talking to a dying man.

"Ne...Never mind how... I got this," Preston mumbled with great difficulty. "...Very valuable. Keep it sa-sa-safe." The old man closed his eyes as even speaking a few words had become too taxing for his dying body. His chest was now barely moving and both Papa Julian and Molly Gertrude knew it was only a matter of minutes before the old man would pass through the valley of death after which he would see the light of paradise.

Papa Julian clutched the book in his hands and stared at Molly Gertrude, not knowing what to say or do. For a moment not a sound was heard, but then Preston rasped and opened his eyes again.

Papa Julian placed the book on the blanket. He took the old man's hand in his and began to pray, but it appeared Preston did not hear him. Instead, he sat straight up from his pillow and for a moment he sat almost erect, while his eyes shone with an unearthly light and held a longing *so* serene and *so* intense, that Papa Julian knew he was witnessing something supernatural.

"They are here," Preston cried out, his voice no longer hoarse and broken, but clearly audible, as if he was back to his normal self. But that was only for a fraction of a second, as immediately after he had said these words, he fell back on his pillow, and all became strangely silent. Not even the ticking of the clock was heard. Even time seemed to have stopped.

Papa Julian did not need to check for a pulse. He knew his friend Preston Linney had entered the heavenly world. He stared at Molly Gertrude, who herself seemed deeply impressed with what they had just witnessed.

For a good while none of them spoke, but then Molly Gertrude let out a small cough and broke through the silence. "You smell that?"

Papa Julian looked up and gave her a small nod. "Flowers," he replied. "I smell roses. They were always his favorite."

Silence again.

Now Papa Julian heard the clock again and outside the window he could hear the twitter of a robin. Things were slowly getting back to normal.

"What are you going to do with that book?" Molly Gertrude asked at last. "You think it really is the first edition of John Bunyan's Pilgrim's Progress?"

Papa Julian shook his head. "I do not know, but it sure looks old, and Preston wanted to make sure I had it. Whether or not it is the first edition I cannot tell, but it is very old, and as such it is of great value. Preston must have believed it is very valuable, for he kept this a secret. He never told me about this book until today."

"Maybe we should not broadcast it to everyone then," Molly Gertrude suggested, "at least not until you know what you want to do with it."

Papa Julian agreed. "For now, I will store it in the basement of our church. I will ask around and see if I can get some knowledgeable people to take a look at it."

Molly Gertrude pressed her lips together and her shoulders drooped. "My condolences," she sniffed. "I know how much Preston meant to you."

"Thank you, Molly Gertrude," Papa Julian replied,

"but at least, my friend is safely home. Of that there can be no doubt."

* * *

The man licked his lips as he peered over the documents before him on the screen of his laptop, trying to force himself to concentrate. But the letters on the manuscript he was reading began to dance before his bloodshot eyes, and the man realized his body just wouldn't cooperate much longer. That wasn't strange, as it was late; way later than he had wanted; but then again, what better time to work than at night when the whole world had finally fallen asleep and had stopped its superficial, shallow and yet monstrous roar?

His wife had gone to bed early. She always did, but tonight it suited him fine. She had still brought him a cup of coffee, black with only one sugar cube, and a peanut butter sandwich. He had not touched either of them. The coffee in the mug with the yellow smiley face and the words, "We love you, grandpa," was cold and stale, and the sandwich had become prey for a couple of irritating flies.

It didn't matter, as he had more important things to worry about than a mere sandwich.

What time was it anyway?

The alarm clock that stood on top of a pile of study books right near the edge of the desk gave him the cold, harsh facts that it was after three in the morning. The man let out a sigh and threw himself back in his swivel chair. So close… He was *so* close to unravelling the secret. But a miss was as good as a mile, and *so close* simply wasn't close enough.

He rubbed his eyes, rolled his chair away from the desk and got up. Maybe if he splashed water on his face he could still study one more document. But he discarded the thought. He needed to stop as he was just too tired.

It was then that his laptop made a beeping sound.

A message.

The sound of the little bell, warning the man of an incoming message, pierced through the silence of the night and reverberated around the room. The man swallowed hard. A message this late? Maybe it was good news, and one of his contacts on Facebook had found out something more.

The man hesitated. He noticed his head was hurting too. Maybe he should just push that one button that would turn the whole caboodle off. Had he not done enough studying for one night? The silk sheets of the king-size bed, right next to the warm and comforting presence of his wife seemed like the better solution. He would turn the computer off and go to bed.

Bleep, bleep.

The warning bell... it sounded again.

The man narrowed his tired eyes and stared at his laptop screen, torn between his desire to check the message and his cozy, comfortable bed.

However, anyone who knew the man a bit better would have known what choice would be made. The man stayed, forced the tiredness out of his system, and plopped himself down in front of the screen once more.

Seconds later, with a driven look on his face, he opened his Facebook page.

Two new messages.

His eyes scanned the page and almost instantly he found what he was looking for. There it was. A message from Sanchez Cippolini.

He had met Cippolini on Facebook some months earlier, but actually had no idea who Cippolini was, where he lived, and what he did for a living, but he didn't really care. That didn't matter. Just about 95% of his contacts on Facebook account were like that; unknown social shadows, and Sanchez Cippolini was no exception. The one thing that had made Cippolini interesting, and what had prompted the man to add him as a friend on Facebook, had been their mutual love for history, artifacts and relics. Cippolini was a real history buff, and now after all those months that friendship on Facebook finally paid off. As the man read Cippolini's message his eyes began to sparkle and he lifted both of his hands in the air in a jubilant fashion.

There it was. A name... an actual name. Preston Linney. The man's eyes feverishly glided over the whole message.

It appears that what you are looking for is in the hands of a man, a pastor named Preston Linney. I don't know where he lives, but you can Google him, and no doubt you will find out all you need.

Good night. Sanchez.

The man grinned.

Preston Linney, huh? He had heard that name before. Wasn't that a pastor in Boulder Valley? If that were true, he didn't even have to pay for expensive travel tickets. He could just go there, and get it over with.

He let out a long, satisfied sigh as he turned off his laptop.

Life was good when everything went your way.

Very good.

CHAPTER TWO

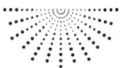

Papa Julian let out a sigh and scratched behind his left ear while staring at the flyer before him on his mahogany desk. The jovial man with the fringe of white hair around his balding head usually carried a happy smile around his thin lips, and it was rare to see him even the slightest bit depressed. He had been Calmhaven's pastor for a long time, and cared for the spiritual welfare of his flock with untiring zeal. It had earned him the title 'Papa'. His real name wasn't Papa, but Julian Maxwell, or Reverend Maxwell. But that name Papa had somehow grown on him. Even the most unbelieving person in Calmhaven had to admit the man had a heart for people, was true to his convictions, and usually quite willing to approach those with a different outlook on life with an open mind. It had even resulted in a good friendship with Malcolm O'Hara, Calmhaven's Catholic priest who was responsible for Saint Mary's Catholic Church, located on the other side of Calmhaven.

One could always hear him say something like, "Smile, you are on candid camera. The Good Lord is watching," and his dark brown face was usually framed with a bright smile for any who came to the door of the church. But today was one of those rare days when his worry lines seemed to have deepened and he was hoping the Good Lord wasn't checking His candid camera.

The day had started out so well.

Blue skies, bright sunshine, and his dear wife Bella had surprised him even before he had gotten up.

"Good morning, Julian," her cheerful voice had sung when she opened the curtains and the light was streaming in. "This is the day the Lord has made. Let us rejoice and be glad in it, and to help you do that, I brought you your coffee."

Dear Bella. Not one step was ever too much for her.

But after he had gotten dressed and told the Lord he

was ready to face the day, things had progressively gotten worse. He just sat down for breakfast when Wolfgang Crossley knocked on the door.

Wolfgang Crossley, of all people.

Bella had let him in.

Of course she had. Hospitality was one of the first marks of a concerned Christian, but Papa Julian was not at all happy to see Wolf, as he liked to be called, and for once he wouldn't have minded if Bella had not been so kind.

Wolf was in a constant struggle with Papa Julian's teachings, he did not let one opportunity pass by without disrupting the Wednesday night Bible study. He had begun to speak against Papa Julian openly, causing doubts in the hearts of two new young members, who had only recently been baptized, but were barely grounded in the word. Wolf didn't think a true believer should ever be sick, or have serious problems, and he should always be wealthy and rich. "It's a promise from God, pastor," he would invariably say. "Goodness and mercy shall follow me all the days of my life." Strangely enough, Wolf's children were often sick and the man himself usually carried a disruptive scowl on his well-groomed face instead of a smile, but at least, and true to his convictions, he had a few cents to his name. He ran Calmhaven's digital printing and advertisement company, SpiderWeb Corporation, and thus he could easily compete with Calmhaven's cream of the crop.

"Good morning, Wolf."

"I just came to tell you, Maxwell, I am through." The man scowled as was his custom, but today he seemed especially wroth.

"Coffee, Wolf?"

He shook his head. "You don't understand, Maxwell. *I-am-done*. I no longer wish to attend your church, and I will no longer give you my tithe."

Papa Julian frowned. "Your tithe? You never gave your tithe to the church."

"Regardless," Wolf bellowed, "I quit."

Wolf was as greedy as he was rich, and money had always been the issue with him from the very beginning. On Sundays, when the collection bag was passed, he usually made a big show of his giving and he dumped a whole bunch of pennies in the collection bag. It would make a lot of noise and he would look around with a smug expression, making sure everyone would know that Wolfgang Crossley was into being generous. But that had backfired one day, and it had been the start of Wolf's disgruntlement with the church. That happened when he realized to his horror one of the coins in between his pennies had actually been a gold coin.

He had wanted to grab it back. He was just about to stick his bony hand in the collection bag when usher Stan Pot stopped him and shook his head. "Sorry, Mr. Crossley. Once in, forever in."

All eyes had been on him, as everyone waited with bated breath to see Wolf's reaction. At last he had grumbled and hissed, "Fine. At least God will give me credit for a gold coin when I stand before him in heaven."

But Stan Pot, not afraid of anything, had again shaken his head. "No you won't, Mr. Crossley. Your heart only gave a few pennies, so that's all the credit you'll get."

From that day onward, Wolf had been disgruntled and today, for some reason, he gave up his membership.

"All right, Wolf. No one is forcing you in our church. I wish you all the best."

But Wolf wasn't finished.

"I found a better church, with a better pastor that's much more understanding," he grumbled.

"I am happy for you," Papa Julian answered as calmly as he could. "As I said, I wish you all the best."

Wolf wrinkled his nose. "Yeah, you can look all smart and confident, but I'll tell you, I am going to do my best to take your treasure away as well."

"Excuse me?" Papa Julian felt a tightening in his chest. "What are you talking about? My treasure is in heaven. My treasure is God."

"No it isn't," Wolf fired back. "You are just like all the other hypocrites. But I just felt I needed to tell you that." After he had said those words he turned around and stomped out of the room, leaving Papa Julian and Bella behind with their minds racing, as they had no clue what Wolf had meant by his ominous warning.

That had been the first downer of the day.

The second one came when Papa Julian went into Calmhaven right after breakfast to take care of some business.

A slender, young woman with blond curls that

seemed to stick out in all the wrong places, and with piercing, blue eyes stopped him in the street and pushed a flyer into his hand. Behind her slightly pursed lips was an inviting smile, so bright it had made Papa Julian uneasy, curious, and suspicious, all at the same time. It was the kind of a smile you'd expect from the salesman at the door, just before he was about to explain the road to paradise in meaningless garble. It was also the smile people would offer when they wanted you to come to a meeting, like a political rally or to some sort of jamboree. Papa Julian was right. The first words out of the girl's mouth confirmed Papa Julian's apprehensions as she sang, "You are invited, Sir. Wednesday night at seven. It will be most glorious."

Papa Julian stared at the young woman. Whatever it was, he was not eager to attend. What's more, on Wednesday night he was supposed to lead his weekly Bible study, this time in Sunrise Acres, the only nursing home in Calmhaven.

Thus, he politely shook his head and gave the girl a smile of his own. "Thank you, Miss. But I am a bit busy that night."

"There's a meeting on Thursday as well, and another one on Friday. There's no excuse," the girl sung back in cheerful tones. "Many are called, but few are willing to be chosen. I am telling you, your life will never be the same after you have heard Pastor Sharlan. He will bring you the words of life."

"Excuse me?" Papa Julian bent forward a little. "Who is Pastor Sharlan?"

The girl frowned and curled her lip. Such ignorance was clearly beyond her. "Pastor Sharlan Tan," she clipped, but almost immediately she forced her almost seductive smile back on her attractive, young face. It was obvious it was her job to lure as many people as possible into whatever meeting this Sharlan fellow was organizing.

She licked her red lips and then added, "You'll love Pastor Sharlan. He is just so anointed, so eloquent, and he holds the keys to a brighter tomorrow."

"Does he now?" Papa Julian scratched his head as he kept on staring at the young woman. He had never heard of a pastor by that name, but something about the whole thing caused him concern. This pastor Tan was apparently a traveling evangelist, but how come nobody informed him the man was coming to Calmhaven? Shouldn't churches work together in unity?

He had never heard of a pastor by the name of Sharlan Tan either, and it made him feel uneasy.

The girl tilted her head a bit to the side and pushed her long, blond curls over her shoulders with a swift movement of her hand. "So... you have never heard of Pastor Sharlan Tan?" she smacked.

"No, I have not," Papa Julian responded a little curtly. "Should I?"

"Well, as I said," the girl continued undeterred, "Wednesday night, the heavens will be opened, and all who come may drink freely of the waters that Pastor Sharlan will pull out of heaven so willingly."

Papa Julian shuffled his feet. "How does he open the heavens, and what will come out?" As the words left his mouth, he realized he must have sounded rather skeptical. "Sorry," he added in a mumble, "I meant no disrespect."

"Pastor Sharlan Tan is God's man for this moment," the girl continued. Papa Julian noticed that when the girl spoke the man's name, her voice dropped to a whisper, as if a sacred utterance had just left her lips. She stopped for a moment and then spoke in soft tones, "Then what did you go out to see? A prophet? Yes, I tell you, and more than a prophet." *

Papa Julian recognized a verse of scripture. These were the words spoken of by Jesus Himself when he was talking about John the Baptist. He licked his lips. "Are you saying that this Sharlan is a prophet of God?"

"Oh yes, yes he is," the girl cried out. "And as I said, he's greater than a prophet. He is the one that will pave the way for the return of the Messiah."

Papa Julian stared at the flyer in his hand and scratched his head. "I am a little confused," he muttered.

"Confused?" The girl's blue eyes became wide. "Then yield to the utterances of Sharlan Tan and you will no longer have to grope around in darkness."

"I am not groping around in darkness," Papa Julian fired back. "I am the pastor of Calmhaven Trinity Church. I just don't understand why this man, Tan or whatever his name is, would just organize some sort of crusade without consulting the pastors of the local community. Don't you think it would be a decent thing to do?" Papa Julian did not easily get irritated, but as his wife Bella could confirm, he was no saint, and had his moments of frustration and anger, and this was one of them. After all, the welfare of the church was of the utmost importance.

The small coat of jovial varnish on the girl's face was scratched. She shook her head and her smile froze. "You are resisting the new," she hissed. "Like many other pastors we've encountered, you too are yielding to your carnal jealousy. You are drinking old, stale wine, wine that's coming out of moldy wine skins. Master Sharlan however, offers the new wine. Pure, undiluted wine that is full of heavenly clarity." Her smile was completely gone now, and instead a mocking scowl hung around her lips. "It's not too late to repent, Pastor. But do not wait too long." She pointed a crooked finger at Papa Julian's belly, and the blond curls on her head no longer appeared to be just messy and unorganized, but looked more like vicious spikes ready to wound and maim. "Those who do not grab the chance when they can, will be gobbled up by the monster of carnality which ultimately leads deep into the pits of hell," she snarled and hissed, and was now pointing to the heavens, as if she were a fiery prophet carrying a message of doom and destruction.

"Well… eh, thank you," Papa Julian replied. "It has been most enlightening talking to you."

All at once, it was almost uncanny, the girl's smile returned. Papa Julian had always wondered what kind of a smile the snake had offered on that fateful day in the Garden of Eden when the deluded creature had tempted Eve, but he was certain it must have been somewhat similar to the grimace that now hung on the young woman's face.

"Goodbye, pastor," she said, and before Papa Julian could say anything she had moved away to someone else who was walking by. She clearly did not want to waste any more time on such an unreceptive soul as Papa Julian.

He stared at her for a moment as she peddled her flyers with zeal, and had slipped back into her supposedly innocent, but insincere sales mode. Within minutes she had delivered at least ten more flyers.

When he came home that afternoon he had not been able to shake the feeling that a storm was coming to Calmhaven. First he'd had that meeting with Wolf, in which the man had threatened to take away his treasure, and now a certain Sharlan Tan was coming to town, and from the looks of it, he was a weirdo. Of course God was in control, and while Papa Julian was well aware of the fact that God would sometimes shake the apple tree, just to see how well grounded His children were in the good, clean earth of God's Word, still this was not his best day.

There was only one thing to do.

He needed to pray.

Thus he told Bella that he would skip lunch, and he locked himself in his study and brought the matter before God's throne.

*Matthew 11:9 NIV

CHAPTER THREE

That night, right after dinner the bell rang. Papa Julian had just sunk into the big leather armchair that Jim Mackintosh, who ran the local furniture store, had sold him. Jim Mackintosh, being a member of Calmhaven Trinity Church, had sold it to Papa Julian as a bargain; at least that's what the man had told him, but Bella had been shocked when she found out how much they still had to pay for the recliner.

Regardless, Papa Julian liked nothing better than to sit down in it after dinner and read his Bible, right near the open fire. Thus, when the bell rang, loud and demanding, he let out a sigh and looked at his wife with a puzzled expression.

"The bell? Who could that be?"

"Expecting anybody?" Bella asked as she looked up from her work of mending a hole in one of Papa Julian's socks.

Papa Julian rubbed his nose. "Not really. Maybe Angelique Fletcher is having her baby. She told me she wants you at her side when the baby is coming. It's her first delivery." He shrugged his shoulders.

Bella smacked her lips and got up. "My father told me marrying a preacher wasn't going to be a bed of roses, and I can understand why he said it. I can't actually remember the last time we had a day off."

Papa Julian knew his wife was right. Sometimes, (no, virtually all the time) the needs of the flock seemed overwhelming, but Bella wasn't complaining. She would support him no matter what, and as she passed by his chair to open the door, he could see the twinkle in her eyes. In passing, she let her hand gently slide over his head. "You are a good man, Julian. Marrying you was one of the best things I did in my life."

"Those are my words," he replied, while a sheepish grin played around his lips. It was one of the things he always said when he agreed with his dear wife. He followed her with his eyes into the hallway, and listened when she opened the front door.

"Good evening, Ma'am," a deep, male voice said. It sounded like a dark, distant rumble in the atmosphere. "Is Pastor Julian home?"

Whoever that was, wasn't coming to inform him that Angelique Fletcher was about to deliver a baby. This voice he had never heard. He put the Bible on his coffee table and stared at the door, wondering who would show up.

He did not have to wait long, as seconds later Bella returned, looking a bit surprised. "There's a gentleman here to see you, Julian."

"Well? Let him in," Papa Julian replied. He flattened the fringe of his white hair, just in case it didn't look presentable.

A man entered.

A man whom Papa Julian had never seen.

He was not particularly tall. Not too tall, and not too short either. Just about average in size. There was a slight smile around his lips, but Papa Julian couldn't decide whether or not his eyes were smiling too. It was hard to tell because of the reflection of the flames of the open fire on the man's face.

The stranger peered around the living room with demanding, piercing green eyes, although, strangely enough, they were not entirely green. There was a bit of yellow mixed in as well. It struck Papa Julian as most peculiar, and reminded him somewhat of the eyes of a wild cat he had been staring at in the Boulder Valley Zoo not too long ago when he went there with the Sunday school children.

And like that wild cat, this man too filled his heart with an unpleasant feeling of dread. There was no denying it, this stranger carried a heavy spirit. He was dressed like a priest, somewhat similar to the outfit his friend Malcolm O'Hara would wear during mass in St Mary's Catholic Church. Like Malcolm, he wore a priestly garment that reached all the way to his ankles and was buttoned up to his neck. But unlike Malcolm, this man had tied a large, purple sash around his protruding belly and he did not wear a cap. Most peculiar was the way he wore his hair. While all the priests Papa Julian had ever met had been either balding or, if they had any hair at all, would be well-groomed, this fellow had long hair, tied back in a pony tail that was glistening in the light of the fire by reason of way too much gel. And he carried more than just a heavy spirit, as around his neck dangled a golden cross with a loop that Papa Julian recognized as an Ankh, the ancient Egyptian hieroglyphic symbol for "life".

At that instant he knew who was standing before him.

This man could be none other than that prophet the girl on the street had told him about. For a long, silent moment both men stared at each other. At last, Papa Julian cleared his throat and while he rose from his seat he mumbled, "Pastor Tan I presume?"

The man grinned and bobbed his head, causing his pony tail to dance around. "I see that my fame has paved the way already." He offered Papa Julian his hand. "And you must be Papa Julian. Melissa told me you wanted to see me."

Papa Julian coughed and shook Tan's hand. "I am not sure I follow you, and who is Melissa?"

"You don't mind if I sit down, do you?" Tan asked. And without waiting for approval he sank down in the seat that was nearest to him. With a flick of his hand he moved his greasy pony tail to the back of the headrest and folded both of his hands together over his belly.

Papa Julian scratched his head again. "Would... would you like a cup of tea?"

Tan shook his head. "Thank you, Julian, but I am not here to indulge myself in the niceties of life. Melissa told me you were upset that I had not contacted you before I came to Calmhaven." He licked his lips and thought for a moment. "Well, here I am. By the way, you may call me Sharlan."

Papa Julian narrowed his eyes. "I take it Melissa is the woman I met on the street today? The one who gave me the flyer that tells me you are having an open air meeting tomorrow?"

"That's right," Sharlan answered with a satisfied grin. "She's a lovely girl, isn't she? Faithful and true."

Papa Julian sat down, not quite sure what to expect. Bella walked over to the back of Papa Julian's chair and placed both of her hands on her husband's shoulders. It felt good to feel the strength of her presence.

"Well, shoot," Sharlan Tan said as he leaned back in his seat while tapping his belly with his fingers, "Ask me anything you want to know. It's my aim to please."

But no questions came. Papa Julian's mind had gone blank.

Sharlan Tan decided to be helpful. "I suppose you would like me to tell you about the reason of my crusade in Calmhaven?"

Papa Julian tilted his head. "I suppose that would be a good start. What *is* the reason?"

Sharlan Tan lifted his eyes to the ceiling and stared for a moment at the antique lampshade that was hanging above his head, as if it would help him to draw strength from above. But then he closed his eyes, blew out a loud puff of air and raised both of his hands in the air, revealing his tattoo covered arms. Papa Julian narrowed his eyes as he stared at the sculptured arms of the man before him. A host of symbols Papa Julian had never seen before.

Almost instantly he spoke, but the tone of his voice had changed. It sounded solemn, holy and dark, all at the same time, and Papa Julian felt the hairs in the nape of his neck rising.

This man, this Sharlan Tan, was a strange man indeed.

"Behold, a storm is coming. A storm that will set apart the sheep from the goats, and that will cause a great widening of the eyes. Hear ye therefore the words of my anointed one, my prophet, who will ride on the wings of the wind and will preach unto you the true salvation. He will pour out the new wine and speak with signs and wonders following. Therefore hear ye him, so you may be pleasing in my sight. By honoring my prophet, you will be honoring me and thus escape the wrath to come."

For a moment it was still as the words, so eloquently spoken by Sharlan, still hung in the air and cast an uncomfortable blanket of oppression over the room. Then the man cleared his throat and finished by saying. "Thus saith the Lord."

He lowered his hands and as the sleeves of his garments fell back over his arms, the tattoos were covered again. Sharlan's eyes were still fixed at the ceiling as if he were saying goodbye to a host of invisible creatures that had communicated these words of questionable wisdom, while an ethereal smile rested on his face.

But Papa Julian's face was not smiling at all. His face wore a concerned frown and he shivered. To him it felt as if someone had forgotten to close the door to the freezer. He leaned back into his seat as far as he could, while treasuring the firm and loving hands of Bella, still upon his shoulders.

When Sharlan was finally done staring at the ceiling, he glanced at Papa Julian, looking somewhat dazed.

He blew out another long sigh and shook his head. "Wow... Wow..." It was all he could muster at first. But then he collected himself, pulled on his pony tail and mumbled, "Every time God speaks to me it's absolutely overwhelming." He whipped out another wow, and cast Papa Julian a grin while waving his left index finger in the air. "Tell me, brother, what can be more invigorating than directly hearing the voice of God?"

Papa Julian started at him with a blank expression.

"Well, there's your answer," Sharlan spoke at last. "This, brother, is what our crusade will be all about."

Papa Julian wanted to say he was not Sharlan's brother, but Bella was one step ahead of him. "We have heard you, Sir... but my husband is not your brother and your utterances are not just confusing, but they are in fact, most disturbing."

Sharlan's eyes widened. Then the smug smile on his face froze and his face darkened. He cleared his throat and when he answered he hissed, "Utterances? You call God's words a mere utterance?" He wrinkled his nose and said. "Let the women keep silence; for it is a shame for women to speak in the church." *

Papa Julian was not easily irritated, let alone angry, but now he felt the fires of indignation rising in his chest. Still he controlled his emotions and said in a calm voice. "My wife may speak wherever she likes, Mr. Tan. What's more, she is in her own home, and I wish for you to treat her with respect and common courtesy and—"

Sharlan Tan interrupted him. Instead of answering Papa Julian, his hands shot back into the air, revealing his tattoos again, and almost instantly he broke forth in another prophecy. "—Behold, let not anger and ignorance stand in the way of the move of my spirit. You, my son Julian are called to play an important role in the furtherance of the kingdom."

"Excuse me?" Papa Julian did not wait for the prophecy to be finished. "I've had quite enough."

Sharlan stopped talking, his shoulders tensed. "You do not want to hear what God wants to tell you?"

"I talked to God this morning extensively," Papa Julian fired back, "and what's more, I've got my Bible, so I am well supplied."

Sharlan shook his head and swallowed hard. "Let me

tell you anyway, for if I do not give you the words of God, they become within me a burning fire." Without waiting for Papa Julian's response he went on and said, "God told me you have great riches to share. You have treasures God wishes you to give to the kingdom."

"What treasures," Papa Julian smirked.

"God showed me a room—a dark room, and I believe it is situated under your church." Sharlan narrowed his eyes as if he stared into the unseen world, "I see a dark basement... I can see it so clearly. It's musty, and inhabited by spiders and rats, but it's there where you store...," he paused, "No, in which you *hoard* a manuscript that God wants you to sell, so the proceeds can go towards the building of my... eh, God's new cathedral." He deliberately raised his brows as he peered into Papa Julian's eyes and said, "Will you heed the commandments of your God, Father Julian?"

"They call me Papa, not Father," Papa Julian fired back. "And I have no idea what you are talking about. I don't believe a single word of what you are supposedly prophesying, and my wife and I have heard more than enough." He pointed to the door. "Goodbye."

"It's a book," Sharlan still cried out. "You have a most valuable book. I can see it now and you must not hoard the riches that have so freely been bestowed upon you."

"Stop your nonsense," Papa Julian's voice skipped a pitch.

Sharlan did not blink as much as an eye and folded his arms over his chest. "It's always the same," he mumbled, while shaking his head. It caused his pony tail to fly around in a defiant manner. "The old church always resists the new church. The old wine skins can never hold the vibrant, sparkling new wine from the heavens."

"Goodbye," Papa Julian interrupted him. He got up from his chair and walked towards the hallway, expecting Sharlan to follow him.

Sharlan smacked his lips and gave Bella a short nod. "I'll leave, but nobody can stand against the plans of God. His plans never fail. You cannot always resist the spirit of the Most High."

"Out," Papa Julian had to fight the impulse to grab Sharlan by the shoulder and push him out the door, but he kept his cool and patiently waited until Sharlan had walked past him and had opened the front door.

"Goodbye Father Julian," the man smirked as he stepped into the night.

"Papa," Papa Julian hissed. "They call me 'Papa'.

"Whatever," Sharlan mumbled. Then he turned and disappeared into the moonless night without saying another word.

Papa Julian stared for a while into the darkness, as if to make sure this man was really gone and then returned to the warmth of his living room and the loving arms of Bella.

"W-What was that all about," Bella said with a quiver and Papa Julian noticed her lips were trembling.

Papa Julian shook his head while he took Bella into his arms and gave her a tight hug. "He said a storm was coming... That was probably the only true thing that false prophet said tonight." A slight headache had risen and Papa Julian felt exhausted as if he had been walking a marathon.

"What did he mean by great treasures in the basement of our church?" Bella asked with a grave expression. "How would he know you have that old book of Pilgrim's Progress that your good friend Preston gave you on his deathbed?"

Papa Julian shook his head. "I do not know, Bella, but I am awfully tired now. Let's commit it all into the hands of our heavenly Father and go to bed. Surely God will know what to do, as He is in charge of even the smallest of details."

*1 Corinthians 14:34-35 (KJV)

** 2 Timothy 3:12 (KJV)

CHAPTER FOUR

Emily Bimbleton couldn't suppress a giggle as she and Billy Thistlewaite ploughed through the fields on the outskirts of Calmhaven. She had almost plunged forward as her foot had gotten stuck under a protruding root, but Billy had put his arm around her. It felt good to feel his steady arm around her waist, and she secretly hoped she would stumble again.

She would never have taken this way herself, but Billy had wanted to take a shortcut. He claimed he had done it before. "If we cross here, it will save us a good twenty minutes." He was certain of it, and Emily believed him. There was no use arguing with Billy anyway, as he was used to doing things his way, and he was often right.

Emily Bimbleton worked as a maid at the farm of the Henderson's, quite a few miles away from Calmhaven, but she needed to go to Calmhaven's Social Security office first thing in the morning. Mister Fairclough, the manager, needed to see her right at 8.30. But that was a problem as the first bus did not pass by the Henderson's until 9.00.

But then there was Billy.

Ruddy Billy Thistlewaite on his moped, who just happened to be visiting Mr. Henderson. Mr. Henderson was about to hire Billy as an extra farmhand, and thus he had hired Billy that day, just to see if Billy's skills were indeed as fabulous as the boy had claimed.

"Just hop on my moped," he had told Emily when he heard of her predicament. "Tonight, when I go back home, I'll give you a ride. We'll be in Calmhaven in a jiffy."

Riding on the back of Billy Thistlewaite's moped? Emily's heart skipped a beat and she couldn't help blushing. That meant she would have to fold her arms around Billy's waist, and maybe she could rest her head against his leather jacket…

"Surely you have somewhere where you can spend the night?" Billy wanted to know.

And he was right. Emily could sleep at her aunt's house, right near the Social Security office.

But Billy had not been right about being in Calmhaven in a jiffy. About ten minutes after they had left, that evening, the moped decided it was time to call it a day. The motor sputtered and stalled, refused to yield to Billy's curses, and after a few minutes died completely, right near a giant oak tree.

In the distance they could see the lights of Calmhaven. It was an idyllic setting. The moon that peered occasionally through the clouds that were drifting by, the light of the stars that smiled down on them, and the soft wind rustling through the leaves; it all set the stage for a romantic moment.

"What do we do?" Emily asked while she looked up into Billy's disgruntled face.

"Walk," Billy said. "We'll have to." In frustration he kicked the front wheel of his moped and then locked it. "Tomorrow, I'll have to fix it, but I can't do anything about it here."

And that's when Billy had suggested they take the short cut.

And he had been wrong again.

Half an hour later they both realized he had made a mistake. Calmhaven still seemed far away, and all that Billy's shortcut had brought them were nasty scratches, a rip in Emily's skirt, and shoes that were soaked as they had accidentally stepped into a swamp. It appeared they had made no progress.

Still, Emily didn't mind.

Being with Billy Thistlewaite, in the middle of the night, while they were struggling forward over the rough terrain was not a punishment. This was one of those nights she would not easily forget. In her mind's eye she could already envision the admiring looks of Conny Hogg and Alberta Duffy, her best friends. "*You* were out with Billy Thistlewaite... at night? You mean, you crossed the fields together and he held your hand?"

"Yep." She would proudly nod her head.

"And... did he kiss you?"

He had not yet done so, but then again, Calmhaven was still quite a walk, and every time she stumbled and fell he had grabbed her arm and gently lifted her back up. At those moments she would smell him. The scent of leather mixed with... She wasn't quite sure what it was, but surely, it was the scent of a man. Surely a kiss was not far away.

"We need to try to find our way back to the main road," Billy's breath was labored. "This is not good. I don't even know where we are."

But it was Emily who knew.

"I know where we are," she said and pointed to the right. "Look over there, just behind that hill, you can see the belfry of Calmhaven's Trinity Church."

Billy peered in the direction Emily pointed, but saw nothing. "You see ghosts," he smirked. Just then the moon shone through the clouds and illuminated the landscape before them. "You are right," Billy exclaimed, the relief clear in his voice. "That's wonderful. In that case we are closer than I feared. I was right after all."

And thus they ploughed on.

First down a hill, then up again and there, stood the church, a the stately silhouette of Calmhaven Trinity Church, fully basking in the light of the moon.

"Almost there," Billy cheered. "That was about time, as my feet are getting tired."

Emily nodded. She knew all good things always come to an end eventually, and she had to admit, she was getting awfully tired as well. Once they were near the church, they were practically in Calmhaven.

But what was that?

Emily stopped in her tracks and peered towards the church. She had spotted movement. Somebody was moving near the church.

"Wait," she whispered, and pulled Billy's arm.

"What?" Billy muttered.

"Did you see that?"

"See what?"

"A shadow. I think there's somebody around the church."

Billy wasn't in the mood. "Of course you see shadows. It's night, for crying out loud, and the light of the moon is constantly casting shadows everywhere."

Emily shook her head. "It's not that, Billy... Look there..." She pointed towards the side of Calmhaven's Trinity Church, now about 50 yards away. "It looks like somebody is doing something there." She grabbed Billy's arm and squeezed it. "Don't you see that? I even think he's limping." Billy narrowed his eyes and peered in the direction Emily had pointed.

"You are imagining things. I see nothing."

"Look again."

"You are right," he hissed at last. "It looks like someone is doing something near the window. What's he doing?"

"Don't know," Emily whispered back, "but it can't be good."

As they both stared at the shadowy figure, a slender, tall person, they could hear the faint sound of a scraping screwdriver, very careful and very methodical.

"I think he's prying away the stained-glass window," Billy mumbled. "Guess, he's afraid that breaking it will make too much noise."

"We have to tell the police," Emily squeaked, and an ominous feeling of dread entered her spirit. "T-There's a burglar in the church." Just as she said it, they saw how the spook was lifting the whole window out of its frame and placing it against the wall of the church. A second later he crawled through the hole and disappeared out of sight.

"A burglar in the church?" Billy grinned, and shrugged his shoulders. "Nobody wants to break into a church. You know what I think?""

"What?"

"It's probably one of those homeless people, or somebody who has lost the right way. It's really nothing to worry about." He narrowed his eyes again and then shrugged his shoulders. "I don't see anything anymore. Maybe we even imagined it, and we just saw the shadows of the branches."

"Of course you don't see anything," Emily smirked. "He's inside."

But Billy wanted to move on. "Come on," he said, "let's go. We still have a ways to go."

But Emily was not convinced. "We have to tell the police. There's a robber in the church."

"Sure," Billy replied in a mocking voice. "You go to the police, but *I* am going to bed." Without waiting for Emily's reply he pulled her by the arm and dragged her forward.

All of Emily's romantic feelings vanished as snow on a sunny day.

She knew what she had seen, and it filled her with dread. Tomorrow, she would go to the police.

Earlier that evening, just before the sun had disappeared behind the distant hills, Grease had made a run to the small homeless shelter of Calmhaven. He was late and being late was bad news in regards to the way the homeless shelter of Calmhaven operated. "We serve meals till seven," Miss Tannenbaum, who ran the shelter with an iron hand had explained, "but if you want a bed for the night, you need to be in by six." He didn't like Miss Tannenbaum very much, but then again, beggars can't be choosers, and the awful reality was that Grease was a beggar, and therefore he just had to abide by the rules of Miss Tannenbaum.

He had not always been a bum, but when his love for the bottle had gotten the best of him, his wife Rita left him and took the kids with her. They had relocated in Boulder Valley. Soon after she'd left he had lost his job and things had gone from bad to worse. First the repossession of just about everything that Rita had cherished had caused conflict. Then the electric company turned off the lights, and finally the landlord had forced him out on the street. "Sorry Grease," the man had said, "but I need to live too. Out you go."

He had not always been called Grease either. That just was his street name. His real name was Gerald Grealy, but when it was clear to the world that he no longer walked the accepted way and he had stopped shaving and caring, people just started to call him Grease.

That was about five months ago, and now he was on the street, moving from garbage can to garbage can, only to find a small measure of comfort at night under the guiding eyes of Miss Tannenbaum.

But tonight that small comfort would not be his. Tonight the poor, stubby man was too late.

It was after six and although he could still count on a plate of grub, he knew Miss Tannenbaum would not allow him to stay the night.

And he was right.

Miss Tannenbaum shook her head when he wanted to enter the sleeping quarters. "No Grease, you know the rules," she said as she cocked her brows. "Food is all you get tonight."

"Bad luck, huh?" Clint Crantston smirked after

Grease had taken his place at the large dining room table.

"Whatever," Grease mumbled back while he waited for his bowl of grub. Clint Crantston was homeless himself, and the two sometimes played a game of chess in the shelter.

"Ask Pastor Julian," Clint suggested. "It's worth a shot." He gave Grease a confident smile while he licked his spoon clean. Grease eyed Clint with suspicion. That was easy to say for Clint. He had a place for the night.

"Who?" Grease asked.

"You know, Pastor Julian. He's the bloke that runs Calmhaven's Trinity Church, and he's a good man. Whenever I am in a fix, I can count on him."

Grease stirred his food with his spoon and thought about it. "I remember that church. When I was still married, I went there a few times with my wife."

"Yeah," Clint said while he pushed his empty bowl away. "It's up on a hill, a bit outside Calmhaven."

Grease rubbed his forehead. "The kids enjoyed their Sunday school, and I remember listening to a few of his sermons."

"Oh," Clint said with a scowl. "Doesn't look like it did you much good, Grease. Anyway, that's my suggestion."

And that was it. The meal was done. Clint couldn't stay, he had to leave.

At first he had not wanted to go down to Calmhaven's Trinity Church. He didn't like the idea. Surely that pastor would remember him. It would be too painful, and he would have to explain to the pastor how come he was in such a state. After all, that man had known his wife Rita and in those days he still wore a suit and tie, as a clerk for Calmhaven's First National Bank. He even vaguely remembered that the pastor had been playing tag one Sunday with all the kids from the Sunday school.

No, it would be better to sleep against the wall of Calmhaven's First National Bank. At least, that place was sheltered from the wind, or maybe he should just rough it for the night, and sneak into Calmhaven Park. People weren't allowed there after ten, but there was only one guard, and the park benches were fairly comfortable.

However, things turned out differently.

When he reached the park, they had closed the gate earlier than normal, and the First National didn't offer much hope either. For some reason a big, fancy police car was stationed right in front of the place that he had in mind. Two policemen were keeping watch while smoking cigarettes. Only God knew how long these fellows were going to stay there.

It was then and there he decided he had to go to Calmhaven's Trinity Church. He would just have to swallow his pride, eat humble pie, and hope for the best.

Making that decision actually felt good. Surely that pastor, being a Christian and all, would open his doors for him, and Grease walked with new courage in his heart towards the area of town that housed the church.

But when he came in the area and spotted the church, he wasn't so sure anymore. Just as Clint had said, it was a bit out of Calmhaven, situated on a small hill. He remembered the church from the times he had been there with Rita and the children. The building had always impressed him. It looked so stately, so clean and fresh with the white washed walls and the beautiful stain glass windows. He really wasn't sure whether or not God existed, but he could imagine that *if* God was real, He would probably live in a place so fresh and clean as Calmhaven's Trinity Church.

The church itself was dark, but there was a small house on the side. That was probably where Pastor Julian lived.

What should he do now?

Just ring the bell?

Hello, Pastor. I used to be a member of your church, but the devil got a hold of me, and now I am a bum. I need a place to sleep... That wouldn't go over too well. What was he even thinking?

At that instant something caught his attention. A noise? A sound? What was it?

He turned and walked towards the church itself. The wind ruffled his messy hair and pulled on his beard.

It was getting cold early this year, and he shivered.

Had he really heard something?

Of course not. His mind was just playing tricks on him. What else could he expect when he was roaming alone through the fields at night, like a scared rabbit hoping for a place of safety.

But then he heard it again. Very softly, as if something was being moved. It was just around the corner of the church. He bit his cracked lips and moved stealthily forward. It reminded him of the times that he, as a child, had been playing Cowboys and Indians in the dark with flashlights as guns. But that had been make-believe. Now he had no friends around the corner that would flash their lights on him and shout a victorious, 'Got you.'

He let his grubby hand slide over the whitewashed wall of the church as he moved forward to the corner. The wall felt strangely cold, almost as cold as his heart.

Now he was at the edge.

He heard nothing. At least nothing that was out of the ordinary. Only the wind in the trees made a howling sound and there was the distant cry of a night owl.

Did he dare look?

Come on Grease. What are you, a sissy?

He bit his lower lip again, and stuck his head around the corner.

Nothing.

Of course not. What did he expect? A bear or a wolf? These animals no longer roamed the fields of Calmhaven.

He heaved a little sigh of relief and stepped confidently around the corner of the church. But as he did, he immediately stopped in his tracks and he let out a muffled curse. He had almost crashed into a stained glass window.

That was weird.

Stained glass windows were supposed to be *in* the wall of the church, not *against* it, and this one was leaning at a slight angle as if to prevent it from falling over. Grease had always liked those beautiful church windows with the exquisite colors that cast such a heavenly light in the church. But what he liked even better tonight was the gaping hole in the wall of the building. The church was dark, but the hole itself was inviting. Almost as if it was shouting out to him, 'Welcome, Grease… Enter into the joy of the church.'

Grease licked his lips. Why was that window out of place? He had no idea. Maybe Pastor Julian was doing some repairs. But whatever the reason, it didn't matter to him. What mattered to Grease was that he could just crawl into the church without having to bother Pastor Julian. And that suited him fine. Now he did not have to explain who he was, and what he had become. He could just climb in, find a warm spot and have a wonderful night.

It wasn't his responsibility either. If Pastor Julian didn't want people nosing around in his church, then he should not leave such inviting holes. It was the pastor's own fault.

Without waiting another second, Grease placed his hands on the edge of the hole and pulled himself up.

Tonight, he would have a wonderful sleep.

CHAPTER FIVE

"Raspberry tea, Dora, or Earl Grey?" Molly Gertrude cast Dora a sideway glance as she looked at her assistant from the kitchen. As was their custom, after the day's work, both women would sit for a while in Molly Gertrude's living room, sipping tea and enjoying each other's fellowship.

This had been going on for quite some time now. Around ten in the morning Dora Brightside, Molly Gertrude's enthusiastic, bubbly assistant, would drive up to Molly Gertrude's home, in her second hand Kia Rio, and together they would drive to the center of town where Molly Gertrude would open the doors of the Cozy Bridal Agency, Calmhaven's only wedding agency. Then, when the work was done, Dora would drive them back.

"Today I think I'll settle for a good, old cup of Earl Grey," Dora answered as she stretched her legs and yawned. Today had been a rather long and taxing day at the office. It always was at the end of the month, as that was usually the day on which they had to check and balance the books, bills had to be paid, invoices were sent off, and there were always a myriad of other nagging details to take care of.

But now it was done and Dora was longing for a good cup of tea, and she was especially looking forward to Molly Gertrude's Citrus Lemon Curd cookies. Few delicacies were as tempting as the old woman's pastries.

"Sometimes I wonder if I can still keep up," Molly Gertrude called out from the kitchen while she poured the steaming, hot water into the teapot. "Most people my age are just enjoying life. They stopped working long ago."

"You *are* enjoying life," Dora replied with a chuckle. "I cannot imagine what you would do if you did not have the Agency. And don't forget, you leave virtually all of the administration to me."

"I know," Molly Gertrude said as she returned to the living room carrying a tray with the tea and, to Dora's joy, a plate of cookies. "But I must confess, days like this do take a lot out of me. In fact, it's been mostly 'just' work these last few months. You know, people marrying, organizing parties, lonely men hoping to find the right partner... but there hasn't been much of,...," her voice trailed off, "...well you know our *other* work."

Dora frowned. "You mean, our sleuthing work?"

Molly Gertrude sighed as she sat down in her easy chair and motioned for Dora to help herself with the cookies. A guilty expression flashed over her face, "I suppose I am a bit ungrateful, am I not? But yes, that's what I mean. That's the kind of stuff that really makes me tick."

Dora reached over to the cookies and took one off the tray. She broke the cookie in half and before she stuck a piece in her mouth, a thoughtful expression crossed her face. "On the other hand, maybe you should be grateful not much evil has happened lately. I mean, what fun is there in a murder?"

"I know," Molly Gertrude said and she took a sip of her tea. "I am an ungrateful, little old lady. Still, it's the truth."

"There's a new novel of Edward Springston coming out," Dora said, trying to be helpful. She knew how reading detective stories was one of Molly

Gertrude's great passions. The book case of the old woman was loaded with all the famous and not so famous novelists who had tried their hands at this particular genre. "If you can't solve your own crimes, you can at least read about somebody who does."

"A new Edward Springston book?" Molly's eyes lit up. "Where did you hear that?"

"It's all over the internet," Dora replied, after which she stuck the second part of her cookie into her mouth.

Just as Molly was about to answer, the phone rang.

The sound was harsh, loud and penetrating, and Dora almost choked on her cookie. She had fruitlessly tried to persuade Molly Gertrude to buy a smartphone, but the old woman stubbornly insisted that there was nothing wrong with her old dial phone and it was unwise to make unnecessary expenses. "Not everything that glitters is gold," Molly Gertrude would invariably say when the subject would come up. "My old phone is still working fine. It does all that it needs to do."

Thus, Dora had given up long ago arguing about it, but she hated the harsh sound of Molly Gertrude's home phone. At least at the office they only used

Dora's phone, which would play the delightful first tones of Vivaldi's Four Seasons.

Molly Gertrude pushed herself up out of her chair and scrambled to the phone that stood on a wooden stool near the kitchen.

"Hello… Molly Gertude's home. How may I help you?"

A second later Dora heard her say, "Pastor Papa Julian… How good of you to call… Excuse me?"

It was silent for some time as Molly Gertrude was intently listening to the voice on the other side of the line, and Dora noticed that Molly Gertrude's face darkened.

"You are kidding? Tell me that is not true."

More silence.

Molly Gertrude now looked alarmed. Dora didn't dare to chew on her cookie, for fear she would miss an important detail. It was clear from Molly Gertrude's reaction that she was upset.

"And… have you called JJ Barnes?"

JJ Barnes? Something was clearly wrong.

JJ Barnes was Calmhaven's main law-enforcer. Molly

Gertrude and Dora had often crossed paths with him in the past.

"No… I am here with Dora," Molly Gertrude continued. She nodded her head a few times and played with the telephone cord.

"Now? Of course. I'll ask Dora if she can drive us."

Drive us?

Dora looked at her watch. It was after six and she was hungry and tired.

"Bye, Pastor." Molly placed the receiver back on the hook and sighed. The conversation was done.

"What is it?" Dora asked. "Please don't tell me somebody got killed again."

"No murder," Molly Gertrude said as she moved back to her chair. "At least, not as far as we know."

"What is that supposed to mean?"

Molly Gertrude shrugged her shoulders. "That was Papa Julian from Calmhaven's Trinity Church. There was a burglary."

"In his house?" Dora's eyes widened.

"No, somebody broke into the basement of his church."

"What's there? Usually basements are not the place where people store important things."

"You never know," Molly Gertrude replied. "I know for a fact that Malcolm O'Hara, Calmhaven's Catholic priest, has some jewel studded crucifixes stored in the basement of his church. They are not very valuable though, but Papa Julian had something of great value stored there, and now it is gone."

"What was it?"

"I told you about that manuscript, remember. Or rather the book that his old friend Preston handed to him."

Dora frowned. "Yes you did, but who cares about a book. It wasn't even an old Bible."

Molly Gertrude shook her head. "You don't understand. It was a very old, ancient copy of John Bunyan's Pilgrim's Progress. Could have even been the first edition."

"You told me, but I never heard of it," Dora answered, feeling rather dumb.

Molly Gertrude peered at Dora. "It's a Christian classic, Dora. It's not a mystery story, but you really should read it sometime. It is an allegory of the journey of a Christian throughout his life all the way up to his arrival in heaven."

"And now it's stolen?"

Molly Gertrude nodded. "And Papa Julian thinks he knows who may have done it. He wants us to come over to his place and discuss it. Would you be willing to drive us there?"

"Who does he think did it?"

"He didn't want to discuss it over the phone, but he said he and his wife Bella had a visit from a real weirdo a few nights ago, and he seems convinced that man did it."

"A weirdo? What does that mean?"

Molly Gertrude finished her tea in one gulp and stared at Dora. "I do not know, Dora, but do you still have the energy to drive over there?"

Dora couldn't help but chuckle. "And you just said it was time for some action, didn't you?" She reached for another cookie and then got up. "Let's go, Miss Molly Gertrude. It seems we are back in business."

Half an hour later Molly Gertrude and Dora sat at

the dining table in Papa Julian's living room. They were both stirring a steaming hot bowl of chili con carne with a spoon. When they had entered the pastor's small, one story house, right next to Calmhaven's Trinity Church, Bella had spotted right away both women were in need of food.

"Have you eaten anything at all," she asked when Molly Gertrude and Dora entered the hall, "you both look famished."

"It's not that bad," Dora chuckled. "I had some of Molly Gertrude's cookies." Bella let out a deep sigh and shook her head. "That's no good, no matter how tasty those things may be. Sit down, and I'll serve you some proper food." Thus they were both served a generous portion.

"Tell me, Pastor," Molly asked in between blowing on her chili, "what happened?"

Papa Julian shook his head in dismay. "It's terrible, Miss Molly Gertrude. This afternoon I went down to the church. As soon as I entered I felt an unusual draft."

Molly Gertrude looked up from her bowl of chili. "A draft?"

Papa Julian nodded. "One of the glass stained windows was taken out of the wall. It was gone."

Molly Gertrude put her spoon down. "You mean somebody smashed one of those beautiful windows?"

"No, it wasn't broken. That's what's so strange about it. It was just taken out. There was nothing but a big, gaping hole in the wall." Papa Julian scratched his temple. "But then when I investigated it closer, it turned out that the stained glass window was carefully taken out of its framing, and was leaning against the wall on the outside."

Molly Gertrude and Dora glanced at each other.

"Most peculiar," Dora mumbled in between two bites of chili.

"It was," Papa Julian went on. "I am glad whoever it was that did it didn't break it. It's a very expensive window and of course, very beautiful." Papa Julian let out a little sigh. "I think the thief was afraid he would make too much noise."

"I doubt it," Molly Gertrude spoke thoughtfully. "It takes skill to take a window out like that. The average thief would not go through such trouble. There are ways in which you can break glass without making a lot of noise, you know." She pressed her chin and then asked, "What else happened?"

Papa Julian wrinkled his nose. "I went to the basement. It's funny, but as soon as I opened the door to the basement and turned on the light, I sensed something was terribly wrong. It was almost as if an evil presence was still hanging on in the basement."

"And then?"

"I prayed, and descended the steps. When I was downstairs I got out my key to unlock the door of the cellar. But I did not need a key."

"Why not?"

"The door was open. Somehow the thief had opened the lock."

"Did he break it?"

Papa Julian shook his head. "No, it still works fine. I don't know how he did it, but he didn't break anything."

Molly took a few bites of her chili and thought about it. When she had swallowed her food she mumbled, "So, we are dealing with a gentleman thief. Here's a man who doesn't like to break things. And then?"

Papa Julian's shoulders sagged. "I immediately went to the place where I had stored the book I got from Preston." He narrowed his eyes and studied Molly Gertrude's face. "Remember… Pilgrim's Progress?"

"I do," Molly Gertrude answered. "And then?"

"I already told you. It was gone. I had put that book in a wooden box, to preserve it from humidity and dust. The box was still there, but the book was gone."

"Was anything else gone?" Dora asked. She had finished her chili and leaned with her chin on her hands.

Papa Julian scratched his head. "Not that I know of. But there really isn't much of real value down there."

For a moment nobody spoke, each contemplating the possibilities. At last, Papa Julian broke the silence. "Nobody knew about that book, except that prophet that barged into our living room the other night."

Bella nodded as she folded her hands around Papa Julian's. "He was really weird. Out of nowhere he gave this prophecy that God wanted us to sell that book and give the proceeds to his organization so he could build a cathedral. Can you imagine that?" As she spoke her voice hardened.

Molly Gertrude crossed her arms. "Tell us about that man.

Papa Julian blinked his eyes. "He's strange. His name is Sharlan Tan, and he claims to be a prophet of God. I think the man is just plain weird."

Bella cleared her throat. "As I said, he's creepy. You should have seen the way he entered our room, so proud and arrogant. He said, he came to promote unity among the believers, but his speech was very condemning, not to speak of these weird prophecies he gave. He gave me the goose bumps."

"I heard about him," Dora piped up. "Isn't he the one that's going to give some sort of open air meeting one of these nights?"

"That's him," Papa Julian said, irritation sounding in his voice. "How did you know?"

"I met a lady on the street. She pushed a flyer into my hands when I was on my way to pick up some donuts from Miss Marmelotte's tearoom. That was a few days ago already." Dora let out a sneer. "It was really rather uncanny as she told me all I had to do was to look up at the snake and my life would change."

"She said that?" Molly Gertrude tilted her head.

"It's probably in reference to that Bible passage in the Old Testament," Papa Julian explained, trying to be helpful. "That was the time when the people of Israel were weak and sick because of sin, and Moses put up a curled snake on a stick. Whoever looked at the snake would be healed. Jesus spoke of it too in reference to faith in Him."

Molly Gertrude rubbed at her brow and stared at Papa Julian. "And that man came to your house? Surely, you didn't tell this man about Preston's book?"

"I didn't have to," Papa Julian replied, while his shoulders sagged. "It was really strange, but all of a sudden he raised his hands and spouted out this prophecy. Some sort of utterance that he claimed was a message from God."

"What did he say?"

"Bella already said it. God had apparently revealed to him that I had a very valuable book, and that it was God's will to give the book to him so he could sell it, and use the proceeds for a cathedral that God had commissioned him to build in honor of his greatness."

"Yes," Bella sneered, "I wonder whose greatness he was talking about. Almost sounded like he was talking about himself. I just don't understand how he could have known about that book."

Papa Julian shrugged his shoulders. "There could be a spiritual component to all of this. After all, nobody knew about this, except for you Bella, and of course, you Molly Gertrude. You didn't tell anyone about this, did you Molly Gertrude? We were supposed to keep this between ourselves."

Molly Gertrude puffed out her cheeks and blushed. "Me, telling anyone? Of course not. My lips were sealed. I mean, I did tell Dora, but she's practically an extension of me, so that's the same as not telling anyone."

Papa Julian's eyes widened. "You knew about the book Dora?"

Dora's face flushed. "Well… eh, I did. Just a little. Miss Molly Gertrude told me about it."

"And…," Papa Julian asked while he peered at Dora, "…did you tell anyone else?"

"Of course not," Dora cringed. "Miss Molly told me it was a secret, so I only told deputy Digby about it. But he can be trusted. He's a good man. He would never tell anyone else."

Papa Julian sank into his chair and grunted. "So, the

whole world knows about it. Maybe Sharlan Tan did not get a prophecy at all, but he had just heard about it from somebody else."

Molly Gertrude grimaced. "The bottom line is that the book is gone. Somebody broke into your church and stole a very precious item. What are we going to do about it?"

Nobody knew what to say and they all stared at each other. Molly Gertrude scraped the last bit of chili out of her bowl and asked Papa Julian at last, "And JJ Barnes? You mentioned you did not contact him yet. Why not? He's got all the legal power."

Papa Julian scratched his head again. "I just wanted to talk to you first, Molly Gertrude. I was hoping not to involve the police."

"Nonsense," Molly Gertrude objected. "This is a serious crime, and JJ Barnes may be a bit rough on the outside, still, he's got his heart in the right place."

Dora's eyes lit up. "And his deputy Digby is really smart."

Papa Julian frowned. "Sure. And only God knows whom he shared his knowledge about the book with."

Dora looked down, but Papa Julian gave her a faint

smile. "It's all right, Dora. Don't worry about it. We all messed up, one way or the other." He turned to Molly Gertrude and said, "I think you are right, Molly. I'll contact JJ Barnes first thing in the morning. Will you go with me?"

"Sure," the old woman answered and motioned with her head to Dora that she should come as well. "And tell me Papa Julian, when did you say these open-air meetings are starting?"

"They have begun already," Papa Julian grunted. "That girl told me the first meeting was on Wednesday, so that was yesterday. There will be another one tonight. I believe Pastor Tan is using the activity field near Waterside Snomp, in the poor area of Calmhaven."

Molly Gertrude raised her brows. "Waterside Snomp?"

"Yes," Papa Julian nodded, "You know, that field where they have the yearly fair, and where they hold the cattle market in June."

Molly Gertrude pressed her lips together. "In that case, I guess we will be very busy tomorrow. Maybe we can go and see the prophet in action for ourselves, but first we will go to see JJ Barnes." Molly Gertrude pushed her empty bowl of chili away and grunted in satisfaction. "Thank you, Bella. That was very tasty."

"More chili?" Bella asked.

"Thank you, Bella," the old woman replied. "This was the best chili I ever had, but if I eat more, I am afraid I will burst."

"I second that," Dora said with a grin.

Papa Julian forced a smile on his face, but Molly Gertrude could see that the worry lines on his gentle face had deepened.

CHAPTER SIX

Sheriff John Joseph Barnes, or simply JJ Barnes to most folks in Calmhaven, was a serious looking police officer. His square shoulders and the muscled arms that stuck out of his short-sleeved uniform shirt gave him the impression of a seasoned price-fighter, and his square face with the sharply chiseled jawbones, the bristly moustache, and the piercing eyes matched the picture. He liked to keep a tight ship in the office, and his frustrated roar could often be heard throughout the whole department, even as far as the lavatory, when things weren't going the way he wanted. Thus, his personnel knew crossing him too much would cause more problems than it would solve.

Simply put, JJ Barnes was a sturdy officer, unbreakable, always in control, and not easily fooled. At least, that's how he liked to see himself. His all-time favorite police officer was detective Columbo from the famous TV show in the seventies. Admittedly that was a bit puzzling, because with his immaculate starched uniform and his bulky torso, he looked nothing like the sloppy detective that constantly outsmarted the most cunning crooks. But somehow it was Barnes' understanding that he was at least as smart as Columbo, and to prove it, he had memorized many one-liners of the show that would frequently stream out of his mouth when he was hoping to impress whoever it was sitting at the other side of his desk.

Of course, not everyone saw him like that. In fact, some evil tongues proclaimed the man had more brawn than brains, was way too impulsive, and had a little too much love for fame and glory.

And some of that was possibly true. Nevertheless, those who knew him better, and among them were Molly Gertrude and Dora Brightside, would be quick to say that underneath that stern mask of the smart, unfeeling police officer, there was a jolly man, close to retirement, who was the only perfect candidate in town to dress up like Santa Claus during the holiday season. Shiny, harmless and bright.

Strangely enough, that's how he looked today as well, even though he was fully dressed in his police uniform, and the golden buttons on his jacket seem to glimmer with joy.

Molly Gertrude, Dora and Papa Julian sat before him on the small, creaky office chairs, and JJ Barnes peered at them from behind his desk with eyes that sparkled and gleamed.

Molly Gertrude tilted her head and glanced at Dora. She could not remember the last time she had seen JJ Barnes this relaxed and happy.

Was it his birthday, was that why the smile seemed to be glued to his face?

"Sorry," Molly Gertrude began, "I suppose we forgot your birthday?"

JJ Barnes picked up a pencil from his desk, leaned back in his chair, and began to chew the wood. "My birthday?" he mumbled. "Why do you say that? That's not for another five months." But then his face cleared up. "But… in a way, I suppose you are right. I had a life-changing experience, so in that sense, you could say that I had my birthday." He grunted in satisfaction. "But what can I do for you all?"

Papa Julian cleared his throat. "I guess it's because of a theft. We want to report a theft."

"Really?" JJ Barnes put both of his hands behind his head. "What got stolen?"

"A manuscript," Papa Julian explained, "...or rather, a book."

JJ Barnes narrowed his eyes. "That's hardly a crime. I don't think I can take my men off their important work of patrolling the streets, just for a book. What was it anyway? A cook-book? A telephone book... A pocket book?" He snickered at his own joke.

"You don't understand," Molly Gertrude stepped in. "This is a very old book. It's hundreds of years old and of enormous value. The thief broke into the basement of Calmhaven's Trinity Church and took it."

JJ Barnes leaned forward and pressed his lips with his left hand. "That does sound like a burglary," he finally said.

"Yes," Dora added, "and we think we know who did it."

A slight smile appeared on Barnes' face. "That always makes solving a case a lot easier. Who do you think did it?"

Papa Julian glanced for a moment at Dora and Molly Gertrude, smacked his lips and said, "Sharlan Tan."

His words hit JJ Barnes hard. Instantly, Molly Gertrude could feel how the atmosphere in the room changed and became cold, almost as if somebody had opened the door to the outside. JJ Barnes rolled his eyes, patted his index finger on the desk and shook his head. "Impossible."

"Excuse me?" Papa Julian asked. "Why is that impossible?"

"For two reasons," JJ Barnes replied. He leaned back in his chair, a smug grin on his face. "Reason one, we have already arrested the man who broke into your church. Reason two, it wasn't Mr. Tan." He leaned forward again and pointed his left index finger at Papa Julian. "Mr. Tan is a man of God, pastor. You, of all people, should know that. Sharlan Tan is a man who knows the way, and who has a heart for the lost souls of Calmhaven."

Molly Gertrude rubbed her brow. She wanted to say something, but she was at a loss for words. She looked at Dora and Papa Julian. They seemed to be as amazed as she was herself.

"Y-You made an arrest?" Molly Gertrude mumbled at

last. "Who is it, and did you find the book that was stolen?"

"I don't know anything about that book," JJ Barnes explained, "but we have the culprit in custody. It's a homeless fellow. A miserable wretch that is now known to everybody as Grease."

Papa Julian let out a small gulp. "I know Grease. His real name is Gerald Grealy. He and his wife used to come to my church, but he had problems with alcohol and when his wife left him he went down real fast."

"Whatever," JJ Barnes continued. "I don't care about his history. All I am interested in is keeping the peace, and he broke the law." JJ Barnes swallowed hard. "Can you imagine, he even went as far as taking out the stained glass window, so he could crawl in and out." He looked up and grinned at Papa Julian. "The Good Book agrees with me. Doesn't it say somewhere that he that doesn't come in the sheepfold through the door, but climbs in some other way is nothing but a thief and a robber?"

Papa Julian's face held the hint of a frown, but he did not answer JJ Barnes.

"Anyway," the policeman continued, "the postman saw him crawling out this morning early, and if that's not enough, we got another witness that saw him climbing in."

"You did?" Molly Gertrude gasped.

They could see Barnes' chest rising in pride. "Digby is just taking her statement, right next door. She's a simple maid, Emily Bimbleton. So this case is solved."

"Except...," Molly Gertrude said, "... where's the stolen book?"

JJ Barnes smacked his lips. "I don't know. You are welcome to ask him yourself. He's in cell number two." He crossed his arms and his disposition changed. "But tell me, why did you think Mr. Tan is a thief. That's a very strong and hurtful accusation."

"Is it?" Papa Julian raised his brows.

"It is," JJ Barnes said, and a dark shadow scowl over his face. "I went to Mr. Tan's meeting last night... As you know, pastor, I am not much of a religious man, but this man, this Sharlan Tan... he is a true prophet of God, if I ever saw one. If you don't see that you still have a long way to go." He specifically articulated the word *long* as he glanced at the three visitors before him.

"But he's weird," Papa Julian objected.

"And strange," Dora added.

Molly Gertrude decided not to say anything.

JJ Barnes wrinkled his nose and his body posture clammed up. He thought for a moment and then said. "He is *not* weird and *not* strange. I saw the miracles, last night, with my own eyes. It's unbelievable what that man can do. I saw blind people walking away rejoicing, I saw the deaf being healed... I've seen it with my own eyes, and I have invested in him."

A sour tang rose up in Molly Gertrude's mouth. "What do you mean you 'invested' in him?"

"Like I said," JJ Barnes fired back. "I invested by buying an Isaiah 54 verse 19 seed from him."

Molly Gertrude's faith in God was her strength, her hope and comfort, but she was not very strong in Bible references and she had no idea what that verse in the book of Isaiah said. Thus she looked to Papa Julian for help.

Papa Julian however seemed equally confused. "What is a Isaiah 54 verse 19 seed?" he finally mumbled.

"You should know," JJ Barnes replied while he

wrinkled his nose. "You are a pastor." His hand disappeared inside his coat pocket and he pulled out a piece of cardboard, the size of a dollar bill. Like a dollar bill, the cardboard was green and held an intricate design with the words *Isaiah-seed* written on it in curly fonts. JJ Barnes's face took on a victorious expression as he showed it, and he licked his lips. "Here's the proof. This seed is anointed and blessed by Sharlan Tan himself."

"Explain," Papa Julian demanded.

JJ Barnes face now held an unrestrained smirk. He considered Papa Julian's question and then said, "After the miracles Sharlan Tan performed, he told us we could all become partakers in the move of this great spirit by investing in Isaiah-seeds. The money he earns will be used to help the poor but we, as the buyers, will reap a great financial harvest when the right time has arrived. There were several anointed seeds for sale. I am not very rich so I only bought an Isaiah 54:19 seed. But there were more expensive ones too."

"H-How much did you have to pay?" Molly Gertrude asked.

JJ Barnes shrugged his shoulders. "Only 100 dollars.

It was not too bad, considering I will receive an abundant harvest when the time is ripe."

Concern flashed over Dora's face. "And deputy Digby, Mr. Barnes, did he go too?"

"No, he didn't," JJ Barnes answered and his shoulders sagged a bit. "He said such meetings weren't for him."

Papa Julian wanted to say something, but JJ Barnes stopped him by raising his hands. "So you see, I do not believe for even a second that Sharlan Tan has anything to do with the theft of a mere book. The man has no interest in such trivial matters."

"And you think this Grease did it?" Molly Gertrude said. "You really think a homeless man would go through the trouble of carefully remove a window and then pick a lock so he could steal a book? That doesn't make sense."

A slight smile appeared as JJ Barnes leaned forward. "He was at the scene of the crime. I agree that there are a couple of loose ends that need to be tied up, but overall this case is clear. But as I already stated, why don't you ask the crook yourselves. I am a bit busy as I have a lot of administrative tasks to finish."

The three friends glanced at each other, the confusion

clearly written on their faces. At last Papa Julian pressed his lips together and said, "Thank you for your time, Officer. I suppose we had best be going."

JJ Barnes nodded. "Glad I could be of help."

They all got up from their chairs and walked towards the door. Just as Papa Julian was about to step out JJ Barnes cleared his throat. "Oh... eh, there's *one* more thing..."

They all stopped and looked with questioning eyes at JJ Barnes.

The man smiled. "Columbo always says that," he hiccupped, "but seriously, you should go and see Sharlan Tan for yourself. There's nothing better than hearing the words straight from the horse's mouth."

"Thank you, officer," Papa Julian said again, and without further comment they stepped out of the office.

As they entered the hallway of the police station, they bumped into deputy Digby. He had just come out of an interrogation room, and was talking to a young woman with long, blond curls and dark green eyes that were constantly blinking.

When Digby spotted them his eyes lit up. "Dora," he said, "how nice to see you." He gave Molly Gertrude and Papa Julian a small and polite nod to acknowledge he had seen them as well, and then turned his attention back to Dora. "What are you doing here?"

They could see Dora visibly blushing. She licked her lips and said, "We are here because someone broke into Calmhaven's Trinity Church and stole an expensive book."

"I know," Digby said with a smile. "Meet Emily Bimbleton." He turned to the young woman beside him. "We already arrested the thief, Miss Bimbleton was just about to go down to the cell block with me to confirm we got the right man. You want to join us?"

Dora looked at Molly Gertrude and Papa Julian. "Great idea," the pastor mumbled, and Molly Gertrude nodded as well.

"Good," Digby said, obviously pleased.

He took out a key, opened a door and guided them all through a narrow hallway to cell 2. "Here's a special window," he explained to Emily Bimbleton. "You can see in, but he can't see out. So the man who is sitting there will never know you have spotted him as the thief. Just take your time, and tell us if you recognize him."

Emily Bimbleton smoothed her clothes and her eyes began to blink again. "It was rather dark and far away, officer," she whispered. "I don't know if I can do this."

"Sure you can," Digby said in a jovial voice. "We understand. We get people doing this every day. Just look, will you?" He reached over to a light switch through which he could control the intensity of the lamps in cell number 2, and darkened the cell a bit. "Similar circumstances," he said as he smiled. "Maybe that will trigger something in your memory."

Emily pressed her nose against the glass.

She looked, and stared, and looked some more. At last she let out a sigh, and shook her head. "It doesn't look like it's him," she mumbled. "Can you ask him to walk around a bit?"

"Sure." Digby pushed on a button in the wall which activated a loudspeaker. "Grease, time to stretch your legs. Let's walk."

Grease looked up, a surprised, fearful expression on his face. "W-Walk?"

"Come on, Grease," Digby replied while he tapped with his fingers on the wall. "Just do as we ask you."

Grease got up and walked around.

Digby stared intently at Emily. She shook her head. "No, it's not him. I believe the shadow I saw in the night was limping too."

"Are you sure? It *has* to be this man. Remember, it was dark." Digby pinched his lips together.

Emily sighed again and this time she shook her head even more firmly and decisively. "It's *not* the same man. The man I saw was slender and skinny. This man is small and round."

Digby was genuinely disheartened. "So you are certain."

Emily Bimbleton scowled at him. "I already told you, officer. Do I have to spell it out to you?"

"Sorry," Digby mumbled, and put his hands in his pockets.

Molly Gertrude cleared her throat. "Excuse me, Miss Bimbleton, but what were you even doing near the church at such a late hour?"

Emily let out an impatient sigh. "I already told this man everything." She motioned to Digby. "I saw what I saw, I did my duty as a concerned citizen, and now I'd like to go home."

Digby motioned with his arm to Molly Gertrude that he indeed knew her story and pointed to the door. "You are right, Miss Bimbleton. Thank you for your time. We are most appreciative."

Without saying another word the young woman stepped out of the room, leaving the others behind.

"So…," Dora said when the girl had left, "… we didn't get much further. What do we do now?

"We will talk to the man in that cell," Molly suggested. She turned to Digby. "Is that allowed, officer? May we talk to Mr. Grealy?"

"You mean to Grease?" Digby replied. "Sure. You can go through this door." He walked over to a bolted door right next to the window and unlocked it.

Grease looked up when the locked turned, and instinctively pushed himself as deep into the wall as he could.

"Can we go in, just like that? Molly Gertrude asked, not wanting to get into an argument with JJ Barnes later.

Digby nodded. "I don't think Grease is going to do you any harm, Miss Molly Gertrude. I wish they were all like him."

Thus, the three friends walked in while Digby stayed behind and kept an eye on things through the window.

Grease stared with fearful eyes at the door to see who would be coming in, but then, when he saw Papa Julian, he lowered his gaze and stared at the floor.

"I think, it's best you talk to him," Molly Gertrude whispered to Papa Julian.

The pastor nodded and walked over to Grease. "Do you mind if I sit next to you on the bench Mr. Grealy?"

The man looked up, his eyes glistening. "Please, Pastor," he mumbled. "I-I wanted to see you, I mean... I needed to see you, but..."

"I understand," Papa Julian said as he placed his hand on Grease's shoulder. "There's no need to be ashamed, Gerald. Not with me, and certainly not with God. We've all sinned and come short of the glory of God."

Grease's eyes widened. "You still remember my name, Pastor?"

"I do, Gerald. I have often prayed for you." He thought for a moment and a slight smile appeared. "Who knows, maybe today these prayers are being answered."

"W-Why are you here, Pastor?"

Papa Julian's bushy brows furrowed. "If I see you like this Gerald, I think the reason is twofold. The first and most important reason is you. The question is, 'what can I do to help you.' The other reason is a book. A book that got stolen out of my church."

"A book?" Grease's face looked puzzled. "I know nothing about a book."

"Then tell me, Gerald," Pastor Julian's voice was barely audible, "what were you doing in my church and how did you get in?"

As Grease told his story it became overwhelmingly clear to all who were listening that Grease had nothing to do with the theft.

"So, you believe me, Pastor?" Grease looked with anxious eyes at Papa Julian. "I don't even own a screw driver. What's more, I would never dare to brake a window in the church, Pastor... It's the honest truth. Of course, I had a few drinks again that night, so my mind is a little fuzzy, but as soon as I was inside the church, I crawled in a corner and went to sleep."

"I believe you, Gerald," Papa Julian patted the man gently on the back. "Now, something else."

"What is it, Pastor?"

"Will you come back to church, Gerald? You don't have to come to the service on Sunday. I can understand you may not want to meet all the others. But you can come privately to my house and we can talk. You need a friend, Gerald, and I'd like to try to be one for you."

A tear rolled out of Grease's eye and landed on his grubby pants. "I would like that, Pastor... Maybe crawling through that hole in your church wasn't a mistake after all."

"No, Gerald," Papa Julian said. "I don't think it was."

"Shall I drive you back to the church," Dora asked after they had left the police station. "Maybe," Papa

Julian said while he rubbed his nose. "However, I wish we knew a bit more about the actual value of Pilgrim's Progress. Maybe the whole thing is worth nothing and we are making more of this than we should."

Molly Gertrude considered what the pastor had said and then her face lit up. "That's an idea," she said, at first more to herself than to the others. "I like that idea. Why don't we go to the Greenacre Museum and talk to the curator? He may give us an indication of the actual value of the stolen book. If it turns out that manuscript is extremely valuable, and now that it is also obvious Mr. Grealy had nothing to do with it, maybe JJ Barnes will treat the matter a bit more seriously."

"Sounds great," Papa Julian agreed, "we need to do something and Mr. Sharlan Tan is still not off the hook. In fact, he gives me the creeps. Look how he's leading JJ Barnes around by the nose. The man is not even religious, but he somehow got him to buy that stupid Isaiah-seed."

Molly Gertrude's face held the hint of a frown. "I am afraid our police friend fell under some kind of hypnotic spell. Imagine what he could have bought with a 100 dollars?" She turned and looked at Papa Julian. "By the way what does Isaiah 54:19 say?"

"That's the thing," Papa Julian muttered. "That Sharlan Tan is a complete fraud, a wolf in sheep's clothing. There is no Isaiah 54:19. Such a verse doesn't even exist. Chapter 54 of Isaiah stops at verse 17, and in some obscure translations at verse 18, but never at 19. The man is a total deceiver." He gnashed his teeth and clenched his fists and proceeded to quote a Bible passage.

Molly Gertrude felt her head getting light. This was getting stranger by the minute. She swallowed hard and looked at Dora. "Let's go, Dora. The sooner we can talk to the curator of the Greenacre Museum, the more we'll know."

Dora clicked her tongue and turned the ignition key.

CHAPTER SEVEN

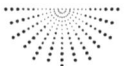

lthough Papa Julian had been to Greenacre Museum many times, Molly Gertrude and Dora had been in the Greenacre Museum only once before, a few years earlier. At that time, the Exhibit Designer of the museum, Jon Wellington was getting married, and had hired the Cozy Bridal Agency to organize his wedding. The wedding had taken place in the garden of the museum, but it had been a disaster as an unexpected rain storm threw a monkey wrench into the works, and all the guests had to be ushered inside. The curator of the museum, Hierro Glyphen, had been extremely upset, fearing for his precious statues, as some guests (Hierro was sure they all had way more wine in their system than they should have had) wanted to touch all the various Egyptian statues and to this day he claimed it was this unfortunate moment that led to his stomach ulcers that prevented him from eating all the foods he wanted.

But, the museum had changed quite a bit since that eventful wedding. Since then, Hierro Glyphen had changed his entire collection, and he now focused on ancient artifacts and paintings. At present, and to his great pride, the museum held the greatest collection of paintings from an Italian school in all of America.

But Molly Gertrude, Dora, and Papa Julian didn't come for the paintings of Leonardo, Tintoretto, and Sandro Botticelli, and no matter how impressive the silent hallways were, and how inviting the spacious rooms where whispering visitors were looking, they went straight to Mr. Glyphen's office.

The curator, a skinny man with a balding head and a nervous twitch that constantly made his nose move up and down, received them hesitantly in his office.

"Not another wedding I hope?" he muttered, the moment he recognized Molly Gertrude and Dora.

"No Mr. Glyphen," Molly Gertrude reassured him with a gentle smile, "no wedding this time."

The office smelled musty and stale. No wonder, as

there was only one tiny window, right near the ceiling and behind Hierro Glyphen's desk. It was closed.

Hierro Glyphen leaned back in his chair and looked at his pancake-sized wall clock above the door. "Make it quick. I am a busy man."

Molly Gertrude nodded. "We know, Mr. Glyphen. We just wanted to ask your opinion."

The man raised his brows. "My opinion? About... what?"

"May I sit down, Mr. Glyphen?"

Hierro Glypen's nose twitched violently, and he cast Molly Gertrude an irritated look. "Sure. Of course."

Molly sat down in the one chair that stood before the man's desk. Dora and Papa Julian kept standing as there was nowhere else to sit.

"Imagine," Molly Gertrude began, "you have a very old manuscript. A book really..."

"So?"

"A book that was written, say, somewhere in the 17th century... an original."

"Go on."

"How much would a book like that be worth today?"

Hierro Glyphen scratched his scalp. "That depends, Miss Grey, on who wrote it and on the condition of the book."

"I am talking about Pilgrim's Progress... a book written by John Bunyan. I reckon you have heard about it, as it sold almost more copies than the Bible itself. Imagine, it's an original copy, and in fairly good condition. How much?"

"P-P-Pilgrim's Progress?" Hierro Glyphen began to cough and choke and beat his chest vehemently to get some air.

Molly Gertrude looked at Dora with some alarm. "Could you please get the man some water, dear?"

Dora jumped up and ran over to a small faucet in the corner of the curator's office.

"It-It's all right," Glyphen mumbled, his face a little red. "I am fine again. Just got something stuck in my windpipe."

Dora still filled up a plastic cup with water and carried it to the man. "Just take a sip, Mr. Glyphen. It will give you relief."

"Thanks," Glyphen squeaked, and gobbled up the

water in one gulp. After he put the cup down again he let out a sigh. "A book that old... that would be a real jewel, a prize for any museum."

"But would it have any real financial value?" Molly Gertrude insisted.

Glyphen gave her a small nod. "Could be. As I said, it would depend on the condition, but I would estimate such a book would easily go for a few hundred thousand dollars. Maybe even more."

Molly Gertrude's mouth fell open and Dora let out a shriek. "That much," Molly Gertrude whispered.

Hierro Glyphen shook his head and waved both of his hands in objection. "It would, Miss Gertrude, but who cares about the money. There's so much more at stake than just dollars." He stroked his throat and grimaced. "All the world is interested in is money. Today's society is just about gain, success, profit and wealth. People don't recognize true value." He leaned back and pointed to the door that led back into the museum. "The paintings, the statues and the amazing artifacts we house here... they are filled with secrets. They are, in a sense, our forefathers. They are the rock from which we are hewn, they cry out their wonders to a generation that is only interested in the digital realities, meaningless thrills like drugs, cheap sex, and lots and lots of money." He narrowed his eyes into tiny slits and added, "I hope you are not one of such pleasure-seekers, Miss Grey."

Molly Gertrude couldn't help but chuckle. "No, Mr. Glyphen, I can assure you I am not. My thrills consist mostly of solving mysteries, which is really the reason I am sitting here before you."

"Good," Hierro Glyphen muttered. "People don't know any more what true beauty is. They are careless, and treat the real treasures of this world without respect." He tilted his head, and waited for Molly Gertrude to continue. Molly Gertrude turned to Papa Julian and raised her brows. "Tell him, Papa Julian."

The pastor cleared his throat. "I had such a book, Mr. Glyphen. I had stored it in the church in a box to prevent it from being eaten by time, humidity and varmints. But somebody broke into the church and stole it."

Hierro Glyphen's face paled. "Th-That is terrible."

"It is," Papa Julian added. "We think somebody stole it and wants to sell it."

"What is this world coming to," Glyphen howled. "Just

as I said. People only think of their material gain." His eyes looked like those of a puppy that had been scolded by its master for chewing on a computer cord. He thought for a moment and then added, "Of course, keeping such a valuable item stored in a wooden box down in the basement of your church, won't help the world much either, as nobody can see it there." He rubbed his nose and while he peered at Papa Julian, he added, "If we recover the book, would you consider placing it in Greenacre Museum? It would be a real asset to the museum."

Papa Julian's shoulders sagged. "Right now I don't have the book, Mr. Glyphen, so it will be hard to make such promises."

Hierro Glyphen gave him a small nod and pressed his lips together. "I understand, Pastor." He turned his attention back to Molly Gertrude. "What can I do? I'll do anything to help you to get your book back."

Molly Gertrude sighed. "Right now, not much, Mr. Hierro. We just wanted to know if such a book is indeed worth something. Now we know."

"Actually, I have a question," Dora said.

Glyphen looked up. "Shoot."

"Did you ever hear of Sharlan Tan?"

Glyphen pressed his lips together in a slight grimace. "Eh... it doesn't ring a bell. Is that some sort of protective sunscreen lotion?"

"He's a man," Papa Julian said while he wrinkled his nose. "A very strange man and we have reason to believe he may have stolen my book."

Glyphen's eyes widened. "Then you should go and see JJ Barnes,"

"We did, Mr. Glyphen," Molly Gertrude spoke up. "But for now Mr. Barnes is unable to take action, so we'll do a bit of snooping around ourselves."

"Oh?" Glyphen said, and he tilted his head. "Any success?"

Molly Gertrude chuckled. "I am sure we'll get to the truth, Mr. Glyphen. We are not planning to let the thief go unpunished."

"You are rather confident," Glyphen spoke through pursed lips. "Maybe this thief is very cunning, and he may even be smarter than you."

"Maybe," Molly Gertrude replied, "that's not all that hard, Mr. Glyphen. I am an old lady, but I know for a fact that whoever he is, he is *not* smarter than God, and God is the One I rely on."

"So does Sharlan Tan, Miss Gertrude."

A shock coursed through Molly Gertrude's body. "What did you say, Mr. Glyphen? I thought you said you did not know Sharlan Tan?"

Glyphen refused to look at Molly Gertrude and rubbed his brow. "Just remembered," he mumbled. "I didn't realize you were talking about that new prophet that came to town. You see, one of my co-workers just asked me advice on a good sun-screen lotion with a high SPF, so when I heard the word Sharlan Tan, my mind just automatically assumed you were talking about such things." He grimaced and his nose twitched violently. "Of course, now I understand you were actually asking about the man."

"I see," Molly Gertrude passed her hand over her face and looked puzzled. "So you *do* know Sharlan Tan?"

"Knowing is a big word," Glyphen muttered. "Like you, he claims he relies on God. But I think he's some sort of prophet. When he came into my office, I thought he was a priest or something. We talked a bit."

"He came to your office?"

"Yeah, he did." Hierro Glyphen squeezed his cheeks with the fingers of his right hand. "Sorry about the misunderstanding." He shook his head in disgust. "The mind is a strange computer, isn't it?" He looked up hoping to get the approval of his three visitors, but they all stared at him with questioning eyes.

"So, when did he visit your office?" Molly Gertrude asked.

"Well… eh, a few days ago." Hierro Glyphen's face darkened.

"And?" Molly Gertrude asked.

"And what?"

"What did he say?"

The question seemed to disconcert Glyphen, and his breath became labored. "Nothing serious. We just chatted a bit. That's all."

"I am sure he did not come to drink tea," Papa Julian insisted. "What did he want to talk to you about?"

Glyphen looked down and fumbled with a pen on his desk. "He said he was raising money for the erection of an enormous cathedral in honor of God. He asked if I wanted to donate a painting, so the proceeds could go to the good cause."

"He asked you that?"

The curator gave a short nod. "He did, but of course I told him no. I could not possibly consent to such a request. These paintings are not mine to give, even if I would have wanted to." He thought about it for a moment and then added, "He's a little strange though. He told me he's staying in a trailer on the outskirts of town. Why would he be living in a trailer? Seems to me, if he's really that important, he should be staying in a hotel."

Papa Julian grimaced. "Maybe he's trying to show how humble he is. After all, our Savior lived in a stable for some time too."

"Did you talk about anything else?" Molly Gertrude asked.

Glyphen smacked his lips. "Nah. As I said, we had a friendly chat. We talked about paintings and statues. He wanted to know about the prices of old artifacts, and asked me where you could find buyers for old things that actually belong in a museum. He said he occasionally bumps into old artifacts that he wants to sell to raise more money for his cause."

Molly Gertrude gave him an incredulous stare. "Go on."

"That's it. There's nothing more. I told him I did not know where you could sell such things. I suggested eBay, but he didn't seem to like that idea. Then he told me he was a prophet, and he gave me a flyer. Some sort of invitation to an open-air meeting he's holding."

He leaned forward and pulled out a grubby piece of paper from under a stack of folders on his desk. "Here it is." He handed the paper to Molly Gertrude. "You can have it."

Molly Gertrude wrinkled her nose. "Thank you, Mr. Glyphen. I don't need it."

Glyphen stared blankly at the paper in his own hand, and put it down again. "Sure, Miss Gertrude. But that's all I know. Honest to God."

"So, did you go to his meeting last night?"

Hierro Glyphen shook his head in a determined way. "Of course not. I already told you, I don't need it. I am not a religious man, Miss Grey. I have no time. I am too busy taking care of my children."

Molly Gertrude frowned. "I didn't know you had any children, Mr. Glyphen.

A small smile appeared on Glyphen's face. "My paintings, my vases, my statues... those are my children, Miss Grey. They take a lot of time, but then again, you wouldn't understand that."

Molly Gertrude smacked her lips. "I do, Mr. Glyphen. Old, classical things are your life. I must say, it's your passion, and these things mean the world to you."

Hierro Glyphen nodded in agreement and sighed. "It's true, Miss Grey. Some people just don't know the meaning of real value." He looked up and concern flashed in his eyes. "Imagine, people just buy and sell paintings, relics, vases... anything, as long as it fills up their pocketbook. But they don't sense the spirit of the ages that lies hidden in between the stone, the paint or the wood." For a moment it almost looked as if he was going to cry. "We need to preserve the true value on this planet, and not let people like Sharlan Tan have his way."

Molly Gertrude chuckled. "That's another thing I can understand." She thought some more about what Mr. Glyphen had said, and then cast him a polite smile. "I guess that just about wraps it all up," she said. "Thank you, Mr. Glyphen." She turned her head and looked at her companions. "Shall we go?"

Papa Julian nodded. "Sounds good, Miss Molly

Gertrude. Thank you for your time, Mr. Glyphen," he said. "You've been indeed most helpful."

"It's nothing," Glyphen said, and he forced a concerned look on his face. "Any time you want my expertise about such things you are most welcome. And please, keep me informed." He shook his head again in dismay and mumbled barely audible, "Such a dreadful crime. How horrible."

Molly Gertrude pushed her chair away and got up. Papa Julian rushed over to support her and the three of them left Hierro Glyphen's office.

When they stepped out of the museum into the adjoining garden a gentle wind ruffled their hair, and Molly Gertrude heaved a sigh of relief. "What a stuffy office," she mumbled. "Everything in there smells about 5000 years old."

"Welcome to the world of the old, stuffy historians," Dora said with a grin.

"Still, I think he's a strange man," Molly Gertrude whispered, " and that's not because he's a stuffy historian. There's something wrong about that man."

"Come on," Miss Molly Gertrude," Dora quizzed. "He seems all right to me. Sure, he's a bit strange, but I wonder what I would be like if I am surrounded daily by portraits of the Ram-headed god of the Nile, and paintings by some Italian painter from the Renaissance?"

Miss Molly Gertrude had to laugh, but she pushed the emotion away. "It's not that, Dora. He's hiding something. I just know it."

"What do we do now?" Papa Julian asked after Dora had driven them all back to the church and Bella had served them each a cup of raspberry tea. "To be honest, I do not even care all that much about that book. I am more concerned about the spiritual influence of Sharlan Tan on the good people of Calmhaven."

Molly Gertrude sipped at her tea and agreed. "He's a wolf in sheep's clothing."

"He's not interested in the spiritual health of the people," Dora added.

"And all he wants to do is to shear the sheep and take their wool," Bella said.

Papa Julian let out a frustrated sigh. "I know all that, but what can we do about it."

"If God be for us, who can be against us," Bella asserted. "We need to ask God to give us wisdom. These things are just too high for us."

Papa Julian cast his wife a grateful smile and nodded. "Thank you for reminding me, dear. At times, I can get so flustered, I even forget the most basic steps of spiritual warfare. Let us pray," he said.

"That's right," Molly agreed. "Let us finish our tea and pray."

Thus it happened that minutes later they fell down on their knees and appeared before the throne of heaven, asking for guidance and wisdom. Even Molly Gertrude, in spite of her arthritis and with the help of Dora, climbed out of her chair and knelt. Then, Papa Julian poured out his heart in a long and desperate prayer. It was so comforting to hear the pastor pray, as he spoke to God with such reverence and respect, while it was equally clear he truly was a friend of the Most High. How could God not honor such a sincere plea from one of His servants?

When Papa Julian was done, nobody dared to even move a muscle, as a wonderful gentle spirit of rest and assurance had come over them. They were steeped in a peace that passes all understanding and the true Shepherd had indeed led them to the green pastures, beside the still waters.

At last they opened their eyes, refreshed, invigorated and full of hope and vision.

"You will not have to fight this battle," Papa Julian was the first to speak, and he quoted a Bible passage. "Take up your positions; stand firm and see the deliverance the Lord will give you. Do not be afraid; do not be discouraged. Go out to face them, and the Lord will be with you." *

"That means," he said, "we do not need to be afraid. We will have to go and see Sharlan Tan, and God will give us the victory."

Bella and Dora nodded enthusiastically, but Molly Gertrude began to feel quite uncomfortable. "Can somebody help me up," she pleaded. "My joints are not what they once were."

*2 Chronicles 20:17 NIV

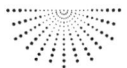

CHAPTER EIGHT

Molly Gertrude had an idea.

After the encouraging verse Papa Julian had received in prayer, they all felt it was time to check out Sharlan Tan for themselves. They should go to Sharlan Tan's meeting. After all, wasn't that what God had put on Papa Julian's heart? *Go out and face them and be not afraid?*

But Molly Gertrude had an unexpected idea. "Yes, somebody should go to the meeting, but how about if some of us snoop around Sharlan Tan's living quarters during the meeting. He's not going to be there, obviously, and who knows, maybe we will find something that will lead us to the stolen book."

"I-Isn't that illegal?" Bella asked, a little pale in the face.

"I am not planning to steal anything," Molly Gertrude replied. "Of course, if I find the stolen book I will take it back, but I doubt I will find it in his trailer, even if he has stolen it." There was a gleam in Molly Gertrude's eyes. "You don't have to do it, Bella. I think it would be best if you go with your husband to the meeting, and I take Dora with me."

A throaty, nervous laugh escaped from Dora's mouth. "It might be dangerous to go to his trailer."

Molly Gertrude nodded. "Maybe, but we are not supposed to cower in the face of danger. Wasn't it Napoleon Bonaparte who said, 'Victory belongs to the most persevering?' "

"Sure," Dora shot back, "he may have said that, but look where it got him, and he wasn't even a man of God."

"Precisely," Molly Gertrude said. "*He* couldn't count on God's help, but *we* can. And, I was thinking about asking asking that young deputy friend of yours to come along..." She let her voice trail off as she glanced at Dora.

Dora blushed and her mouth hung open. "D-Digby? You want him to come too?"

"Of course," Molly Gertrude sang. "You are right when you say it may be a bit dangerous, so it's always good to have the law on our side."

"You think he would even want to come?"

"Of course he will," Molly Gertrude snorted. "Every time we bump into that young man he seems to only see you, Dora. It's my hunch, he'll be overjoyed to watch over you on such a mission."

Dora was won over. A victorious smile had replaced the dark doubts that had flashed over her face only minutes earlier. "I'll call him right away," she said, as she pulled out her mobile phone.

Molly Gertrude had been right as far as Deputy Digby was concerned. He was overjoyed with the prospect of accompanying Dora and Molly Gertrude on their quest, and since he was not on duty that evening, the young man with the boyish grin and the blond curls arrived right on time at the house of Papa Julian, where Dora filled him in on what was happening.

When he heard about Sharlan Tan's antics and what Papa Julian thought of him, he shook his head in disgust and his eyes turned cold. "I don't see what JJ Barnes even sees in him. Imagine that, he even bought one of those silly cardboard papers. He called it his Isaiah-seed, or something like that."

Dora chuckled, and while she wrinkled her nose she said, "I know. He told us. It only cost him $100."

Molly Gertrude overheard them, and a grave expression covered her face. "Don't underestimate the charm and the hypnotic power some people seem to have over others. It's always a mistake to underestimate the enemy. What's more, I think we are dealing with the powers of darkness, and if we are not vigilant and sober, we may fall for the deception of the devil as well."

Digby pressed his lips together and gave her a short nod. "You are right, Miss Molly Gertrude. It just seems so incomprehensible that someone as down to earth as JJ Barnes would fall for someone like Sharlan Tan. He's not even very religious."

"Sharlan Tan may be a crook, but he's not dumb and actually he is very cunning and clever." Molly Gertrude dry-washed her hands and looked at the clock. "We will go over to his place when the meeting has started. I hope that most or even all of his helpers are at the meeting as well so we have free sailing."

It stated on the flyer Sharlan Tan's open air meeting would start right at seven, which was in half an hour.

Papa Julian could hardly wait. He constantly glanced at his watch, and finally, at 6.45, he grunted, gritted his teeth and mumbled, "All right Bella, this is it. Time to go."

Molly Gertrude looked up and motioned for Dora and Digby to get up as well. "Then, we will go as well."

Digby had done a bit of research and found out where Sharlan Tan had positioned his trailer. Sharlan Tan had officially contacted JJ Barnes ahead of time, and arranged with him for a place to camp out. Barnes had cleared a patch of land for him, not too far from the grassy spot in Waterside Snomp where the meetings were held.

Actually, according to Digby, there were several trailers, as the pony-tailed prophet had his crew of faithful helpers, and they obviously didn't all fit in one trailer.

Digby couldn't help but chuckle. "You won't believe where JJ Barnes put them."

The others looked up. "Where?"

"The Dump," Digby grinned. "I guess JJ Barnes wasn't thinking too highly of Sharlan when the man first contacted him."

The Dump had been originally a part of Waterside Snomp, but it had earned itself that glorious name, as it really was Calmhaven's dump. It housed the local junkyard and was also the place where people could get rid of their garbage. It was typically one of those areas that was nobody's responsibility.

Not that the place did not have any potential, but it would need a major overhaul, and few people were willing to invest in it. Even so, there were still people living in scattered, rickety houses with sagging roofs, mostly surrounded by abandoned buildings with planks hammered in front of the doors and windows

Papa Julian scratched his head. "I bet you JJ Barnes is feeling a little ashamed of himself now," he said with a chuckle.

"He is," Digby confirmed. "There are plans to move him and his crew to a better spot tomorrow."

"Which is why it is good we check out his place

tonight," Molly Gertrude added. "Tomorrow, it may be more difficult. At least we can rest knowing there are not too many prying eyes in the Dump." She looked at Dora and motioned her with her eyes. "Ready to go?"

Papa Julian stopped them all with his hand. "Wait," he said. "Let's not go without God's blessing. We should say a little prayer."

They all agreed, and thus they formed a small circle in the pastor's living room and held hands.

"Dear God," Papa Julian spoke with reverence, "into Your hands we commit this evening. Vindicate us, your servants, keep and protect us, and we ask that Your angels will keep us in the way, lest we dash our feet against a rock. Amen."

After the prayer he looked up, the fires of conviction clearly visible in his eyes. "Let's kick this pig," he said and minutes later, they were on the street. While Papa Julian and his wife disappeared around the corner, the others climbed into Dora's Kia Rio, and as soon as they had buckled their seat belts, Dora started the engine.

* * *

Before long they arrived in the area of Waterside Snomp. Here, Dora had to take a right to go to the Dump.

Molly Gertrude and Dora had been there before, but it was not a neighborhood they treasured visiting. On the right, they passed a grubby looking gas station, and there was a bar too, with a crooked sign that read, "Girls, Girls, Girls." It was clearly in business as they could hear music coming out of the place and a scantily dressed woman leaning against the wall while chewing gum. Right next to it was a small night store with a grimy window that was badly in need of a good scrub. The paint on the door was peeling. Molly Gertrude figured the store and the bar kept each other in business.

"The city council hasn't been able to figure out what to do with this area," Digby said, as if it was his fault the place looked the way it did. "If you ask me, it would be best to bulldoze all these buildings to the ground, and build something that would benefit the community. You know, sport fields, a swimming pool… there's so much that could be done with this area."

Molly Gertrude shrugged her shoulders. "Politics, no doubt," she mumbled. She wanted to add something, but Digby told Dora to stop the car. "You see that building over there?" He pointed to a rather high building situated on a corner. Most of the windows in front were broken, and iron stairs led all the way up to top of the building.

"That's a lovely place," Dora said, not able to conceal her disdain. "That place looks gloomy. What's there?"

"Behind that building is the field were Sharlan Tan and his crew are stationed. I figured it would be best to park here, just in case there is still somebody in the camp."

"Good thinking," Molly Gertrude commended Digby. "Let's wait another fifteen minutes, though. The sun is about to disappear behind the hills and it will be dark soon. Let's make use of the cover of darkness."

Dora agreed and parked the car right next to the building with the broken windows. For a moment they all sat in silence, waiting for the sun to go down.

"Music," Dora suggested. "Let's see if there's a good song to keep us inspired." She leaned over to the car radio, pushed a few buttons and began to search for her favorite radio station.

She did not get very far, as almost immediately a

loud and demanding voice filled the car. "Sowing, sowing, sowing. That's what we do to be growing, growing, growing."

Molly Gertrude froze. "Who is that?"

"Don't know," Dora mumbled, and went on with her search. "I'll look for some music."

"No," Molly Gertrude stopped her. "Put that back. Could it be Sharlan Tan?"

Dora swallowed hard and turned the button back. There was the voice again, and they all tuned in to what the man was saying.

"I can promise you that tonight, those of you who will take the plunge and show themselves courageous in the sight of God, and will invest in the kingdom and sow their dollars, will reap a harvest so enormous that there will not be room enough to hold the increase."

"It's true," Digby sneered. "That's Sharlan Tan. JJ Barnes let me listen to a tape yesterday. He must have bought some airtime on Calmhaven's radio station, CH-FM 40."

"Ssshhh."

"But before we sow, I will plow the fields of your

hearts with signs and wonders, so you may know my promises are true and trustworthy." Sharlan Tan almost sang the words.

Molly Gertrude cringed. "So that's the man himself. He sounds smooth."

They all listened for a while to the words of Sharlan Tan. They were eloquent and well chosen, and soft as butter, sweeter than candy. At last Molly Gertrude wrinkled her nose. "I don't like it one bit. Turn it off, Dora."

"You don't want to hear more?" Dora asked.

Molly Gertrude shook her head. "It makes me sick. Turn it off, Dora."

Digby agreed. "This man is a smooth-talker, but it does seem he knows how to deliver a good talk."

"So does Papa Julian," Dora fired back, "but I know he's sincere in his desire to help the flock. This man is nothing but a ravenous wolf, dressed up like a harmless sheep." She gritted her teeth and looked outside. "Time to go. It's getting dark."

They all climbed out of the car and peered around the corner of the abandoned building.

"Look at that!" Molly Gertrude gasped.

"Amazing," Dora added, and Digby was speechless.

For there on a deserted grassy field, littered with paper, cans, bottles and bushes stood three enormous, shiny, slick motor homes, neatly parked next to each other. In spite of the setting of darkness they were clearly visible, as a great array of colored spotlights, empowered by sun panels attached to the roofs, bathed them in a curious light. Molly Gertrude guessed these giants were somewhere between 40 and 60 feet in length and they were custom-engineered body and chassis. Even though at first glance it looked somewhat like a bus, it was clearly so much more. The only words that aptly would describe them were luxury motor-homes.

"What a strange sight," Molly Gertrude muttered at last. "You would not expect something so fancy in such a horrible place like this. No wonder JJ Barnes is going to have them move tomorrow."

The motor home in the middle was even larger than the other two, and they guessed that one was Sharlan Tan's motor home. It was confirmed when they read what was written on the side in elaborately spray-painted, golden colored letters. It read: *Sharlan Tan, your friend in need.*

"You see what it says?" Molly Gertrude mumbled

with a scowl on her face. The others nodded. "He really thinks he's Mister Big."

"H-How much do you think something like this would cost?" Digby stammered.

Molly Gertrude shook her head. "I have no idea, Digby, but it's abundantly clear that Sharlan Tan has more money than he knows what to do with."

"I don't understand," Dora moaned. "Why would someone with such wealth even want to steal a mere book out of the basement of Papa Julian's church? It doesn't make any sense."

Molly Gertrude shook her head. "Who can know the depth of human greed, Dora? I must confess, it is baffling, but to some people enough is never enough. And remember, Papa Julian mentioned Sharlan Tan wants to build a cathedral as well."

"I wonder what these beasts look like from the inside," Digby shook his head while he spoke. "But I guess, we'll never know. I expected some old clunkers with rotten window frames and a rusty chassis, but this is a different ball game altogether."

Molly Gertrude cast Digby a questioning look. "We should at least see how far we can get. I didn't come here to admire the man's motor home."

Digby smacked his lips. "We can't break into a thing like that, Miss Molly Gertrude. That would be highly illegal. After all, I *am* a police officer. If we even scratch as much as the lock, it will already cost me more than my monthly salary."

Molly Gertrude sighed. She knew Digby was right, and as long as JJ Barnes was still waving his so-called Isaiah-seed around hoping to rake in an abundant financial harvest, it was unlikely they would get a search warrant.

Dora agreed. "Nobody leaves a setup like this behind without a sophisticated alarm system installed. I bet you that the moment we even touch one of those bumpers, all hell will break loose."

"What shall we do?" Digby asked.

Molly Gertrude did not know. She had felt the definite leading from God, so she could not accept that this was as far as they would get. She looked down at the ground, closed her eyes and whispered a silent prayer. *Dear God, please open some door.*

She had not even finished speaking the words and the door of the largest motor home opened up and a tall, husky man climbed out.

Our three friends instinctively moved back around the corner.

"What's he doing?" whispered Molly Gertrude, who was the only one who could not see.

"Don't know," Digby mumbled back. "He seems to be fixing something."

"Dora…," Molly Gertrude spoke in a decisive voice.

"What, Miss Molly Gertrude?"

"This is our chance. Walk up to that man."

A visible shock went through Dora's body. "Excuse me, Miss Molly Gertrude. I don't think I heard you correctly."

"Yes, you did," Molly Gertrude replied. "Walk up to him, before he goes back in. Talk to him… It's all by faith. I believe God is going to do something."

Dora turned back and glared at Molly Gertrude. "What do I say to him?"

"I don't know. Whatever, anything. Who knows, but anything is better than hiding behind this dirty wall like a bunch of scared rabbits."

"W-Why don't you go," Dora objected.

Molly Gertrude smacked her lips. "You think that

man is going to want to talk to his grandmother? But he might fancy a talk with you. Just put on your charms and see what happens. In the worst that could happen, he tells you to get lost, but nothing ventured, nothing gained."

"I think she's right." Digby said. "It's worth a shot."

Dora firmly pressed her lips together and thought about it for some time. At last she nodded. "All right. I will do it, but tonight, when this is behind us, you'll bake me a whole tray of Citrus Lemon Curd cookies."

Molly Gertrude couldn't help it, but she burst out laughing. "That's a deal, Dora. Now hurry up, before that man goes back into the motor home."

CHAPTER NINE

Molly Gertrude watched with bated breath as Dora walked up to the motor home. "Hello," they could hear her call out, and she was waving her hand in the air to grab the man's attention.

"You think Dora is going to find out something?" Digby whispered.

"Let's wait and see," Molly Gertrude replied. "I just prayed for God to open a door, and while I was yet speaking, the door of that motor home opened up. I know it doesn't look very logical, but then again, we have no other choice."

Digby grinned. "I start to see why Dora likes to work with you. You are not afraid of the devil himself."

"Of course, I am not," Molly Gertrude spoke back through gritted teeth, and almost a little too loud. "The devil can go fly a kite."

They could still see Dora, but the man was out of sight. "Hello," Dora cried out again. "Anybody there?"

At that instant the face of the man appeared again. He was hard to see, but was partly illuminated by one of the spotlights on the roof of one of the other motor homes. He seemed surprised to see Dora walking up.

Now she was standing before him and they were talking.

"What's she saying?" Digby asked, his voice strained.

"I don't know," Molly Gertrude whispered back. "My ears are not that good. Dora is at least a good 50 yards away." But she did hear something else. A soft pounding noise. Do you hear that, Digby? She looked back at the deputy.

"What? You mean that pounding?" He tried to smile, but his face was full of worry lines. "That's my heartbeat."

Molly Gertrude gently touched Digby's shoulder. "Don't worry, Digby," she tried to reassure him. "Everything is going to work out fine."

Just as she had said it, they saw Dora and the man walk off, away from the motor home, further down into the field. It appeared they were actually chatting, as the man was waving his arms around as if he were telling Dora a story.

"Where are they going?" Digby whispered.

"Don't know..., but you know what?"

"What?"

"The door to the motorhome is still open."

"So?"

"The door *is* open. Let's go in."

"What? That's absolutely crazy."

Molly Gertrude turned around and looked into Digby's face. "Excuse me?"

"I-I..." Digby stammered, "I meant no disrespect... it's just that..."

"What is it Digby? We believe this Sharlan Tan is a crook, a thief and a liar. He's already got your chief JJ Barnes hoodwinked, and even as we speak, he's doing his utmost to rob, steal, and maim the flock of God. The only thing that is necessary for evil to triumph is that good men do nothing."

Those words hit home.

Digby clenched his teeth and nodded. "You are right, Miss Molly Gertrude. The worst that can happen is that he sees us and then I can show him my police badge."

"Good man," Molly Gertrude praised. "Just hold me, will you? I may need your support on this grassy land that is covered with stones and rubbish. Spraining my ankle is not a good idea."

Digby took Molly Gertrude by the arm. They both appeared from their hiding place and stumbled as fast as they could towards the open door of Sharlan Tan's motor home, all the while looking to see if Dora and that man were already on their way back.

But nothing happened.

Dora was not anywhere in sight and before long they reached the motor home.

Digby pulled gently on the door.

It creaked.

"What if there's somebody else in there?" he spoke in low tones.

"We'll tell him we saw the door was open," Molly Gertrude replied. "Go in… quick."

Digby now opened the door all the way and pulled himself up. He stuck his head inside and called out in a muffled voice, "Hello… anybody home? Police!"

No answer.

He turned around and offered Molly Gertrude his hand. "The coast is clear. We can go in."

Seconds later they both stood in Sharlan Tan's motor home. While they had been amazed at the way these vehicles looked from the outside, the inside was even more of a shock.

How could a place on wheels be so spacious? The soft spotlights that caressed the grey colored interior gave the whole place an almost magical outlook, and for just a moment both Molly Gertrude and Digby stared wide-eyed at the scene before them. This was not a room, or a place to sleep, this was a penthouse on wheels.

The floor was partly covered with soft, white deep-pile carpet that looked more like the fur of a polar bear than like the regular carpet one could buy in the cheaper stores. On the places where there was no carpet, like in the kitchen, the floor was made of grey colored wood.

On their left was an actual bar, with stools and a great assortment of liquor, and wherever they looked they were faced with luxurious, comfortable chairs that could be put in any desired angle. The hand rubbed maple cabinet doors provided style, substance and storage, and all the way at the back, was a huge oak door, most likely the entrance to the holy of holy's, Sharlan Tan's bedroom. Everywhere in the ceiling, right next to the lights and the built-in air conditioner were speaker boxes that played Indian music. The place was jaw-dropping, but weird at the same time.

"What now?" Digby asked. He looked at his boots and hesitated. "I feel I need to take off my shoes in a place like this."

Molly Gertrude giggled. "I'll take mine off," she said. "We don't want to mess up Sharlan's nice carpet, do we? You just stay here by the door and keep watch."

"You really think you will find the stolen book?"

"It's unlikely," Molly Gertrude said as she stepped into the heart of the motor home. "I do not know what I am looking for. Clues I guess."

"Whatever you do, hurry up." Digby licked his lips and peered nervously outside into the darkness, while Molly Gertrude stepped further and took everything in that she saw. She was trained in spotting things of interest, but wherever she looked, she saw no Pilgrim's Progress, and not anything that would tie Sharlan Tan to the theft.

Now she passed by the kitchen area. Next to the kitchen and leading up to a door that would most likely be the entrance to the driver's seat, was an artfully designed desk. The wood was cut in the form of a wave and right on top of it was a notebook.

It didn't look special.

It was just an ordinary notebook that came from an ordinary store, and yet something about it caught Molly Gertrude's attention.

"There's a notebook here," she called out to Digby.

"Sure," Digby whispered back. "Just hurry up, all right."

"I am just taking a look."

The cover, in sloppy handwriting, read: *Sermons.*

She opened it.

They were all handwritten notes, probably written by Sharlan Tan. Utterances, prophecies and other such things. It was difficult to read Sharlan Tan's handwriting.

Molly Gertrude leafed through the book. Nothing spectacular.

But then, just as she was about to put the notebook back, she came to the second half of the book and a shiver went through her body. These were more than ordinary notes. These were plain weird.

Use fear. Always use fear. Fear works well with a predominantly catholic audience, but with the right prophecies they may work well with unbelievers, and the so-called born again Christians as well. Fear equals donations.

The word donations was underlined. What was Sharlan Tan talking about? Molly Gertrude's hands began to tremble as she read on.

Since everyone hates sickness, play it out. Convince the audience God does not want them to be sick. Wealth, health and stealth are my weapons.

. . .

Sharlan Tan had drawn a red arrow that lead from the word *weapons* to the right margin in which he had written: "Good for Calmhaven. Use with power. This was unbelievable. These notes contained Sharlan Tan's strategies for his unholy meeting.

"Do you have a cell-phone, Digby?"

Digby frowned. "Me? Of course. Why do you ask?"

"With a mobile phone, you can make pictures, right? At least, that's what Dora told me."

"Sure. You want to make pictures of the interior of the motor home?

"No," Molly Gertrude said. "I want you to make a few pictures of these pages in this notebook here." She took the notebook and walked over towards Digby.

Digby peered outside again. There was still no sign of Dora. "I hope Dora is all right," he mumbled while he pulled out his mobile phone.

"She's fine," Molly Gertrude said in reassuring tones. "Now you see those pages here?" She pointed to several of the pages in the back. "Make pictures of those."

"All right," Digby said and he switched on his camera.

Not a minute later they were done. Molly Gertrude

took the notebook again, and walked back to where she had found it.

"All right, Digby," she said, barely able to suppress the excitement in her voice. "At least one of our missions is accomplished. We did not find the stolen book yet, but I am absolutely convinced Sharlan Tan is a fraud. Let's get out of here." While leaning heavily on Digby's arm, she slid back into her sensible shoes, and seconds later Digby helped her out of the motor home.

"The proof is right in his own notes, Digby," she spoke, while trying to catch her breath as Digby moved her faster than was actually good for her.

"Tell me later, Miss Molly Gertrude," Digby said. He first wanted to get back to the safety of Dora's Kia Rio.

"You got the key?" Digby asked Molly Gertrude when they reached the car.

"Look under the chassis, near the muffler," Molly Gertrude beamed. "Dora always keeps a spare key there in case she locks herself out or loses the key."

Molly Gertrude was right, and seconds later they climbed into Dora's cozy Kia Rio.

"And now, we'll just wait for Dora," Molly Gertrude spoke softly.

"I don't know," Digby wasn't convinced. "What if she's in danger? Maybe I should go look for her. After all, I am a police man."

Molly Gertrude wanted to tell Digby one more time that he did not need to worry, but right then there was a knock on the window.

They looked up into the face of Dora, but she wasn't smiling. A concerned look was on her face and she motioned for Digby to roll down the window. But what was behind Dora filled both Digby and Molly Gertrude was dread, as there, behind Dora, looking equally dark stood a man, husky and broad shouldered. He did not need any introduction. It was the man that was in charge of guarding Sharlan Tan's motor home.

Molly Gertrude narrowed her eyes as she peered at the man.

Something stuck out from under his leather jacket. Molly Gertrude wasn't entirely sure, but she had seen such things before. That man had a gun stuck in his belt.

CHAPTER TEN

"Papa Julian was surprised to see how many people were streaming in to hear Sharlan Tan speak. How was it even possible he had not even heard the slightest rumor of these meetings, as clearly, the whole thing was quite well organized, something which could not have been done in a matter of days.

The only conclusion Papa Julian could come to was that Sharlan Tan had been working on the sly and in secret, thus minimizing any possible objections to his presence.

The whole place was surrounded by a metal fence, and everyone had to pass through some sort of entry gate with a make shift ticket office.

"We have to pay to get in," Papa Julian whispered to

Bella as they took their place at the end of a queue of people wanting to get in. "I thought the word of God was for free."

"Maybe this isn't the word of God," Bella remarked a little dry, and Papa Julian couldn't help but chuckle.

A young couple, standing in line before them, was discussing the event.

"You won't be sorry you came, George," the woman said. She had short stumpy hair, and wore ripped jeans with a loose-fitting sweatshirt that sported an enormous Q.

Her friend, a biker with a black leather jacket with a skull on the back, just grunted. "I don't know, Vivian. You know, I don't much care for preachers."

Vivian had clearly been at these meetings before. "I promise, George. Last night, someone got up from a wheel chair. Just like that… and, eh… did you bring the money, so we can buy an Isaiah-seed as well?"

George seemed doubtful. "I did," he groaned, "but before I hand over my precious dollars, this fellow better delivers."

"He will, George, he will."

Papa Julian stared at Bella and she stared back at

him. Papa Julian was a firm believer in prayer, and had even personally experienced healings by faith.

Once he had discovered a painful lump on the sole of his foot. That was a few years ago already. The doctor had not been very encouraging. "It's not looking good, Maxwell," his message had been. "We will take a sample, and send it to the lab, but prepare for the worst."

Bella had placed Papa Julian on a prayer list, and several members of his congregation, including Molly Gertrude, had fasted and prayed for him.

Two days later, when Papa Julian had awakened from a beautiful dream, the lump was gone. Just like that.

When the doctor called him into the office later that week, ready to give him the bad news that indeed the pastor's health was in serious jeopardy, Papa Julian had broadly smiled at him and shown the doctor the soles of his foot.

There was not a trace of the disease. The doctor had scratched his scalp in disbelief and mumbled something like, "I've never seen something like this. It's not possible."

Thus, Papa Julian was convinced the miracles that

happened in Bible times could still happen today. But he was doubtful they would happen today on a muddy field in Calmhaven, where you had to pay an entry fee to get in, and you would be guided by the words of a strange quack like Sharlan Tan.

"Papa Julian," a youthful voice interrupted the pastor's musings. "How wonderful to see you. Do you want two tickets?"

Papa Julian's eyes widened. "Archie," he exclaimed as he stared at the young man in his early twenties that was occupying the seat in the ticket office. Archie was dressed in a T-shirt that read *Sharlan Gives Tan.* "What are you doing here?"

"Working for Mr. Tan," Archie replied. "He pays me a little bit too, so that helps to pay my studies."

"I missed you at the last two Bible studies," Papa Julian's shoulders sagged a bit.

"I know," Archie said, but I am with Sharlan Tan now. Steven is too."

A dark shadow entered Papa Julian's heart. Archie Carmichael and Steven Mote had just recently joined the church. They both were students; good kids and all that, but they had a bit of a history, and required some guidance.

They had been dabbling with drugs and the occult, but Papa Julian had gone through great lengths to help them, and recently they had both been baptized.

"You need the Word, Archie," Papa Julian said. "Are you all right?"

"I am fine, Papa Julian. Sharlan Tan gives me lots of the Word." He proudly pointed to his T-Shirt. Sharlan gives me my Tan, Papa Julian."

Papa Julian nodded. "Nice shirt, I guess," he said. "Did Sharlan give it to you?"

"No Sir," Archie replied. "I bought it. It costs twenty dollars, but all the money goes to good causes so it's worth it. You want one too?

"No, thank you," Papa Julian said while he stroked his throat and grimaced. "Okay, Archie, how much do I owe you for the tickets?"

"Ten dollars," the boy said.

Papa Julian's eyes widened. "Ten dollars? Just to get in here?"

The boy blinked. "Sorry, Sir," he mumbled. "That's what it costs, and as I said, every penny goes to good use."

"Where's Steven?" Papa Julian asked, not able to hide

his scowl, while he pulled out his wallet. The boy shook his head. "Don't know, Sir. He's somewhere. You can recognize him by the same T-Shirt, although most men that work here are not really part of Sharlan's crew. They are just hired workers."

"Thanks, Archie," Papa Julian rasped as he handed the boy the money.

Just then Wolf appeared.

He literally stepped out of nowhere and stood broad-shouldered and wide-legged in front of Papa Julian. "And... where do you think you are going? He barked.

Papa Julian rubbed his chin. "Wolf? What are you doing here? Will you please get out of the way. I want to hear Sharlan Tan for myself."

"No, you are not," Wolf fired back. "Now, you are on *our* turf, and here *we* make the rules."

"Excuse me," Papa Julian waved with his hands. "This is ridiculous. Why can't I go in and hear Sharlan Tan for myself?"

"Because," Wolf howled, "you are not interested in the message. You are one of the critical ones. People like you bring bad vibes. It disturbs the atmosphere, for you are only interested in preserving your own little kingdom. Did you ever hear that verse in the Bible about pouring new wine into old wineskins? That's what's at stake here, Maxwell."

"Are you some sort of security guard?" Papa Julian asked. "Isn't this a free country?"

"It is, and it isn't," Wolf shot back.

"I see," Papa Julian curled his lips. "I take it that Sharlan Tan is that new, better pastor you told me about a while back?"

"You guessed it," Wolf laughed, and his eyes became dark. "I am now in the inner circle. Mr. Sharlan Tan, with his blessed, prophetic gift, already knew you would be coming tonight. He ordered me to keep an eye out for you. And, as always, he was right."

Bella pulled on her husband's sleeve and whispered, "Let's go, Julian. This place is crazy anyway."

"Sure, Bella." Papa Julian acknowledged her plea, but he was too fired up to turn around and leave.

"So… I can't come in?"

"Nope."

"Not even for half an hour?

"Nope." Wolf tilted his head and pointed towards the gate. "There's the exit, Maxwell. Goodbye."

Papa Julian shook his head in disgust and turned back to Archie. "Can I have my money back?"

The boy nodded and grabbed a ten Dollar bill, but Wolf stopped him. "Oh, no, Maxwell," he cackled, "Once in, forever in. Isn't that the principle on which you operate your church?" A sickening laugh burst from his throat. "Goodbye."

"Let's go," Bella urged her husband. From the tone of her voice it was clear she was afraid Papa Julian was about to do something that would be considered rather unchristian. "Just let these people stew in their own juice, Julian."

Julian gritted his teeth, stared one last time in the face of Wolf, while he cried out to God. "Help me, dear God." At that moment, he was considering giving the man a good punch, or at least a big shove. But instead of resorting to violence, a strange peace came over him. All at once, Papa Julian recognized it as the presence of God, and he knew with great certainty that God was in control. He did not have to fight in his own strength. God would fight for him. All was well.

Even Wolf seemed to sense the change that had

come over Papa Julian, as his left eye began to twitch and he lowered his gaze to the ground.

"Goodbye Wolf," Papa Julian said in a calm voice and turned around. "Goodbye Archie. Give my greetings to Steven."

"I will, Papa Julian," Archie mumbled. The boy was clearly confused.

As they squeezed back out of the gate, Bella mumbled something about this not being the work of God.

"You are right," Papa Julian mumbled when they were outside again. "That's why it will fail. But we will commit ourselves to prayer and leave it all in God's hands."

"I was afraid you would hit Wolf," Bella said as they walked in the direction of their home.

Papa Julian chuckled. "I think I could have. But the Spirit lifted my anger. As I stood there a verse of Scripture came to me and it filled me with peace."

"Which one?" Bella asked.

"It's in the book of Acts. "And now I say to you, keep away from these men and let them alone; for if this plan or this work is of men, it will come to nothing."*

Bella smiled. "Very appropriate. Let's hope Molly Gertrude and her crew got better results than we did."

"I love you Bella," Papa Julian said with a cheerful smile. "Here on earth, you are the best thing that ever happened to me."

"Love you too, Julian," Bella replied, and she took Papa Julian's hand in hers as they walked home.

*Acts 5:38

* * *

While Digby rolled down his window, Molly Gertrude saw how the young police officer felt for his own firearm, hanging right next to him on his belt. Surely, this night wasn't going to end up in some sort of shoot-out? Molly Gertrude peered out the window at the man that was standing behind Dora. His face was partially hidden in the darkness, but it was clear from his build he was strong. But, not only did he look strong, that pistol, clearly visible by the light of the moon, was most disconcerting. Molly Gertrude shivered. *Dear God, please protect us.*

But then, and to their great relief, Dora did not seem to be in the least perturbed.

As soon as Digby had sufficiently opened his window, she leaned forward and greeted them with a victorious smile. To Molly Gertrude, it was as if the sun broke through the clouds on a gloomy day.

"Why are you guys looking so nervous?" Dora chirped in cheerful tones. "I bring you good tidings."

"You scared us," Digby snorted. And who is that?" He motioned with his head to the man that was still standing behind her.

"That's Elvis," Dora stated, as if it was common knowledge. "Let me introduce you to Elvis, as he's got some interesting stuff to share with us." She turned around, and asked the man in a relaxed tone, "I actually don't know your family name."

The man pressed his lips together and stepped into the light. He had his greasy, black hair combed backward and stared at Molly Gertrude and Digby with shifty, nervous eyes. She guessed he was in his early thirties, and wore a too-tight T-Shirt that read, *Sharlan Gives Tan*. It showed his muscles and it was clear he was not somebody to mess with. He forced a weak smile on his face, and said, "Maduro. My family name is Maduro." But then, when he took a better look at Digby he hesitated.

Dora noticed his insecurity. "Don't worry, Elvis," she said. "Yes, that is Digby. I told you he's a police officer, but he's all right."

Digby swallowed hard and narrowed his eye. Molly Gertrude could hear him thinking, "*Is that all I am to you... all right?*"

She tapped Digby on his knee with her hand, and gave him a reassuring nod. "Dora told us she brings us good tidings. I want to hear them." She leaned over and asked Elvis directly, "Tell us, Elvis, what can you tell us?"

"I haven't got much time," Elvis cautioned, "but I met Dora here, and she told me that she is investigating Sharlan Tan." He cast her an admiring look. Digby began to loudly clear his voice.

"We *all* are investigating," Digby snarled. "I see you have a pistol. Can I see your license?"

Elvis blushed, but Molly Gertrude came to the rescue. "Never mind, Digby. That's not the issue for now. Let us hear what Elvis has to say."

Elvis pressed his lips together, gave Digby a scowl, and shook his head. "I've said it all to Dora. She knows." He looked at his watch and gritted his teeth. "I must go back to the motor home. The meeting is going to be over soon, and Sharlan will return."

Molly Gertrude's face dropped, but Dora gave her a reassuring look. "Don't worry, Miss Molly Gertrude. He told me lots of interesting stuff."

Elvis nodded. "Everything I told her is true, but don't tell anyone that you got it from me." Then he turned to Dora and stared into her eyes. "Can I see you again," he asked. "Maybe dinner in town tomorrow night?"

Dora blushed. Digby's ears got red too, but for an entirely different reason. "No, she cannot," he snapped. "She's needed for the investigation."

Dora nodded and gently touched Elvis' arms. "I suppose he is right, Elvis, but thank you so much. You have been an amazing help."

Elvis seemed to be in doubt, but at last he nodded. "Goodbye Dora."

"Goodbye Elvis," Dora said.

The guard turned around, and walked over to the motor home.

"Next time I see you," Digby still called out after him while leaning out of the window, "I want to see your license. Otherwise I will still lock you up... Do you hear me?"

Elvis turned and glared at him, while making a strange sign with his fingers. It made Digby fume, but Dora saved the situation by slipping her arm around Digby's shoulders and she began to gently squeeze them. "Don't get uptight, dear Digby. Besides you, there's nobody I am interested in. I just used my natural, God-given womanly charm, and it worked. Without a doubt, I have discovered Sharlan Tan is a big fraud and a deceiver."

"And so did we," Molly Gertrude exclaimed. "Let's get back to Papa Julian's house. You can tell us all about it on our way there. No doubt, he's about to return as well, and maybe we can put all the puzzle pieces together."

Digby slipped out of the driver's seat and made room for Dora, while he plopped himself down in the back. "Let's drive, Dora," he said. "I can't wait to hear what this Elvis fellow told you."

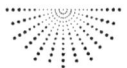

CHAPTER ELEVEN

Minutes later they arrived at Papa Julian's place. It was quite a surprise to find out Papa Julian and Bella had returned long ago. Instead of observing Sharlan Tan and his miracles, they had spent their time praying.

"What happened, Papa Julian?" Molly Gertrude asked when they had made themselves comfortable.

"Wolf was there."

"Wolf? You mean Wolfgang Crossley from our church?"

Papa Julian smirked. "He's no longer a member of our church. He came by the other day and gave up his membership, telling me I am a lousy pastor..."

Papa Julian stared down at his hands, "...but yes, that's the Wolf I am talking about."

"What did he say?"

Papa Julian wrinkled his nose. "He wouldn't let me in. Told me I would disturb the holy atmosphere, and thus I would make it hard for Sharlan Tan to operate."

Molly's eyes widened. For a small moment it was silent, but then they all burst out laughing.

"That's ridiculous," Dora said at last.

"He joined forces with Sharlan Tan," Papa Julian continued, "and he convinced those two youngsters that we were ministering to, Steven Mote and Archie Carmichael, that Sharlan Tan has more to offer than Calmhaven's Trinity Church." He pressed his lips firmly together and muttered, presumably more to himself than to the others, "It's dreadful. I have really failed those young boys."

Then he asked in a flat, monotonous voice, "I thought at first Wolf may have been the thief, since he told me he would take away my treasure. I now realize he wasn't talking about that book at all, but about Archie and Steven. My heart truly yearns for them." He let out a deep sigh, and then asked, "And the book? Did you find it?"

"No book," Molly Gertrude replied, "but we did find out something else."

"What is it?"

"We have proof Sharlan Tan is a fraud and a deceiver."

Papa Julian looked up. "You do?"

Molly Gertrude gave him a firm nod, and told the pastor about the notebook she had found. "That man is no prophet. He is just a very skilled and charmed speaker, who knows how to manipulate the crowds. Digby made pictures of some of the pages in his notebook. If you read those you'll see he does not hear from God at all. He's only making all that stuff up in the hopes of emptying people's pockets."

Papa Julian scratched his head. "But there are people who claimed he performed actual miracles. I heard people were healed from blindness and all kinds of afflictions."

"God is in the business of miracles," Molly Gertrude said. "He is the same yesterday, today and forever,* and he still heals people, except He doesn't need folks like Sharlan Tan to do it."

"His so-called miracles are all fake," Dora added. "I met one of his guards."

"Yes," Digby mumbled, barely audible, "a nice fellow, I suppose. His name is Elvis."

"And?" Papa Julian arched his brows.

"He is sick and tired of Sharlan Tan. His conscience is bothering him. He told me Sharlan Tan is only interested in money and not in the people at all. According to Elvis, Sharlan Tan uses volunteers that he pays good money."

Papa Julian bit the inside of his lip. "When there's a special event, I have to use volunteers too. What's wrong with that?"

"You don't understand, Papa Julian," Dora explained. "He's using volunteers to act as if they are sick, when they are really not sick."

The pastor let out a little squeal. "H-How does it work?"

"For example," Dora explained, "there's apparently a lady on Tan's team who can't see very well, but she's *not* blind. When Sharlan Tan is on stage he claims in a loud and holy voice that the spirit has revealed to him there's a blind person in the crowd that God wants to heal. Instantly, the lady jumps up, cries out that she is that lady, and with the help of some other folks, she stumbles forward. It's not hard to imagine what happens afterwards. And then, right after the miracle, Sharlan Tan begins to push his Isaiah-seed business. The money streams in."

Papa Julian slapped his own cheek as if he wanted to wake up out of a bad dream. "He's that bad?" A frown covered his face, "Why doesn't anybody stop him?"

"Only his most trusted co-workers know about it, and he pays them good money."

Papa Julian winced. "Surely Stephen Mote and Archie Carmichael wouldn't fall for that? They may be weak in the faith, but they are good boys. Even Wolf wouldn't be that dumb."

"They don't know about it, Papa Julian," Molly Gertrude explained. "Most of the people on his team are just hired helpers, people he drops as soon as they leave town."

Papa Julian pressed his fist against his mouth and puffed out his cheeks. "Unbelievable, just unbelievable." Another thought came to him. "And the stolen book? Did you find any evidence of the book?"

"We have still no proof about what happened to the book," Digby said. "But, it will only be a matter of time."

Papa Julian leaned back in his seat while rubbing his forehead. "I feel sick," he mumbled.

"What do we do now?" Bella asked.

Molly Gertrude closed her eyes for a moment, and thought about it. "Tomorrow night is Sharlan Tan's last meeting," she said at last. "Then he'll be off and gone forever."

"I know," Papa Julian moaned. "It's terrible. The book is gone, and we are left behind to clean up his mess."

Molly Gertrude gave a snort. "Remember you got that verse, about not being afraid and that God would be fighting for us?"

"Of course, but what does that mean for us now?"

"That verse still holds," Molly Gertrude replied. "We have to give God room to move." Her eyes shone with conviction. She turned to Papa Julian and as she lifted her finger, she said, "*You* may not be able to visit the meeting, but *we* can. Sharlan Tan doesn't know us, so Wolf will not stop us. Let's put God on the spot, and trust that He will do something out of the ordinary to stop this man. After all, He did promise we did not need to fight in this battle."

Papa Julian considered Molly Gertrude's words, and at last he nodded his agreement. "Sounds good. You are right, Molly Gertrude. It's all by faith. Let's make room for God to work it all out."

As they had made their decision and planned out their course of action, a gentle spirit of peace came over the room, and they all felt the comforting presence of God's Spirit.

At last, Bella got up. "Tea, anybody?"

"A good cup of raspberry tea would be wonderful," Molly Gertrude said, and the others agreed.

* Hebrews 13:8 KJV

* * *

When the friends arrived at the meeting place the following evening, it turned out Molly Gertrude had been right.

No one stopped them at the gate. They didn't see Wolf, and young Archie Carmichael was not around either. Nobody bothered them.

This time, the ticket office was being occupied by a young fellow with a disinterested look on his face, who was constantly yawning. Molly Gertrude had never seen him before. He was wearing the same T-Shirt she had seen Elvis wearing and he took her $10 entry fee with a blank stare. Het put it away and motioned with his hand she needed to hurry up.

Seconds later they were inside on the grounds that Sharlan Tan had rented for the occasion.

"We just wasted $30," Digby fumed as he put his wallet back into his coat.

"Whatever you spend it will be repaid," Molly Gertrude said, and she cast him an encouraging smile.

Digby frowned and stared at her, not comprehending.

"It's from the Bible," Molly Gertrude explained. "It was the Good Samaritan who said that. He told the inn-keeper that he would repay him all the extra expenses he would have to make in taking care of the situation. In other words, God will look after your purse."

"Hope so," Digby answered, apparently not so sure. "I

don't like to spend even a nickel on the likes of Sharlan Tan."

Molly Gertrude scanned the terrain. In front of them was a giant circus tent. Molly Gertrude estimated it would hold at least 2000 people. She had heard that quite a few people had attended the meetings on the previous nights, but today interest seemed low. At least that was a good sign.

Loud worship music rolled over the grounds from two giant loudspeakers that were strategically placed near the entrance. It wasn't a live band, probably just a CD or something like it, but it was way too loud. The guitars were screeching and grating, and it was impossible to even hear the lyrics to the song. Certainly not the type of worship music that Molly Gertrude was so fond of.

"I think I may need a few Advils," she muttered, but Dora had seen something, and pulled on her sleeve. "Look, Miss Molly Gertrude. Over there."

The old woman followed her gaze to a little hot-dog stand not too far from the entrance of the circus tent.

A hot dog stand, right near a religious meeting? She shrugged her shoulders. "The world runs on money,

Dora," she said with a sigh. "Hot dogs, books, T-Shirts… whatever sells."

"It's not that," Dora said. "Look who is eating a hot dog."

Molly Gertrude peered towards the stand.

"What? I don't see what you see."

"That man leaning against that tree near that Port-a-John. What's he doing here?"

Now Molly Gertrude saw it too. "That's Hierro Glyphen from the Greenacre Museum," she exclaimed. "You are right. He said he had no time to go to a place like this, since religion wasn't for him."

"Shall we ask him what he's doing here?" Dora asked.

"Good thinking," Molly Gertrude agreed and they walked over to the man who was just wiping his mouth with his handkerchief.

"Mr. Glyphen," Dora said in jovial tones. "We had not expected to see you here."

Hierro Glyphen swallowed hard when he saw who was approaching, but he forced a little smile on his face and said, "Just checking things out. That's all."

"Weren't you too busy taking care of your children, Mr. Glyphen?" Dora asked.

The man cast her a painful look. "I am. But my neighbor told me this Sharlan Tan is praying for people and that there are occasional healings."

"And you need healing, Mr. Glyphen?" Digby said with a grin.

Hierro Glyphen flinched. "Who are you?"

"He's our friend, Digby," Dora stepped up. "He's helping us with the case of the missing book. He's a police officer."

Hierro Glyphen's nose began to twitch. "I see. In any case, I came here to see if this Mr. Tan could do something about my arthritis. It's getting increasingly worse."

Molly Gertrude nodded in sympathy. "I understand, Mr. Glyphen. Arthritis can be a painful disease. I've got problems with it myself."

"Have you now?" Hierro Glyphen seemed happy to lead the discussion away from police officers and the stolen book. "I was thinking to ask Mr. Chan if he could pray for me. It doesn't hurt to try, and maybe he can do something about it."

Molly Gertrude shook her head. "It's not going—"

But she was interrupted by a loud voice over the microphone. "Good evening, ladies and gentlemen," a suave voice washed over the terrain. Sharlan Tan was beginning his meeting. "Sowing, sowing, sowing," he shouted. "That's what we do to be growing, growing, growing."

"I heard that yesterday on the radio," Molly Gertrude sneered. "He's quite original. We had better find a place in the tent."

"Welcome, welcome, welcome," Sharlan Tan's voice continued, while Molly Gertrude, Dora and Digby entered the stuffy tent. "For those of you who are here for the first time, my name is Sharlan Tan, and I have been instructed by the Most High to be at your service tonight."

Molly Gertrude was surprised to see the attendance was rather small. Only a quarter of the tent was filled up. "It seems the novelty of a new prophet wears off quickly," she whispered to the others as they found a place in the crowd. Sharlan Tan was walking back and forth on the stage, making wild gestures with his arms, presumably to inspire the people.

So this was Sharlan Tan.

As Papa Julian had said, he was dressed in priestly garments and wore his hair in a ponytail. To Molly Gertrude, he looked weird, almost like a clown, but at the same time he carried a certain authority, and she could not deny he had charisma.

Behind him on the stage, on simple stools, sat what Molly Gertrude figured were his henchmen. She counted three of them, one of them she knew; Wolfgang Crossley.

Even though Wolf had apparently joined the inner-circle, still he looked not nearly as threatening as his two colleagues.

They were grave looking, muscled fellows, that did not in any way, shape or form give the impression they were the trustworthy, angel-inspired sheep of God you would expect in a place like this. And, to Molly Gertrude it altogether felt more as if they were being ushered into the presence of a crime boss. She scowled as she stared at the scene. How was it even possible that Wolf, once a faithful member of Calmhaven's Trinity Church, had gotten himself mixed up with Sharlan Tan?

"I don't like it here," Dora whispered. "I hope God is going to do something rather soon."

"We'll just have to wait and see," Molly Gertrude whispered back. "Let's be patient."

As Molly Gertrude scanned the crowd for familiar faces, she spotted JJ Barnes not too far away from the stage. For some reason the man looked a little sour.

"Your boss is there too," Molly Gertrude whispered to Digby. "He doesn't look too happy. His Isaiah-seed has probably not yet brought him the fat, abundant harvest he was promised."

Digby wanted to say something, but was interrupted by the squeal of the microphone, and Sharlan Tan continued with a booming voice.

"What did you go out into the wilderness to see? A reed swayed by the wind?"

Molly Gertrude leaned over to Digby and whispered, "He's quoting the Bible here."

"If not," Sharlan Tan continued. "What did you go out to see? A man dressed in fine clothes? No, those who wear fine clothes are in kings' palaces. That's not me. But there's one in heaven who can abundantly supply above and beyond that you are able to hold."

"Liar," Molly Gertrude muttered under her breath, as

she recalled the shiny, luxurious motor home that Sharlan Tan was traveling in.

"Then what did you go out to see? A prophet? Yes, I tell you, and more than a prophet." Sharlan Tan paused and glanced over the faces before him. "Tonight, I will bring you a message of hope from the heavens. But first the house rules. There is still a limited quantity of Isaiah-seeds available, that you may purchase. In case you are here for the first time and are not yet familiar with the power of these blessed seeds, I will explain them to you in a minute. But let me already encourage you to not let this golden opportunity pass you by. After all, tomorrow I will no longer be around as the spirit has urged me on to spread the Good News."

Digby gritted his teeth and whispered to Dora, "Good riddance to bad rubbish."

"But what about the stolen book?" she whispered back. Digby shoved his hands into his pockets and shook his head. "Maybe we'll never find it."

Sharlan Tan now lifted one finger and waved it around. "In case you want to know more, or would like to make a donation to the ministry outside of buying Isaiah-seeds, you can meet up with my devoted helpers." He turned around and pointed to the three bullies, who gave a wolfish smile. "They are more than willing to assist you with any further questions."

"Brother Tan, can you pray for me?" An unshaven man who was holding a whiskey bottle in his right hand, not too far from where our friends stood, cried out in a desperate, high-pitched voice. "I can't beat the liquor... Please pray for me."

"And me?" An extremely fat woman near the back of the tent, called out, "I need to lose weight."

Sharlan Tan smiled. "What an eager audience we have tonight. You people give me no time to introduce myself." He smoothed a few wrinkles on his robe, rearranged his purple sash, and continued. "But you are right, dear friends. I am here to bring healing. Except, and I hope you understand, I can't pray for you all. I must be guided by the spirit. Remember, even in the days of our prophet Jesus, he only healed certain people. Only the ones that the Father in heaven told him to heal got the actual healing. It's the very reason I give out the Isaiah-seeds. These seeds have been anointed by the spirit, and carry the power to help you, even if I do not pray for you tonight."

"Heal me, Brother Tan. I need it," another old lady cried out. "I am worthy."

"No, I am worthy," someone else raised both of his hands and moaned loudly. "Heal me first."

Sharlan Tan raised both of his hands, and urged the people to be still. He closed his eyes and whispered a prayer into the microphone. "Heavenly father, help your power to come down. Speak to me, and tell me who needs healing tonight."

For a moment he stood motionless. Then he opened his eyes and said, "The spirit told me there is a man out here who is blind. His first name… it starts with a…" Sharlan Tan narrowed his eyes and looked up at the roof of the tent, "…it starts with a… B. The B is followed by a U… Buzz, maybe?" He rubbed his nose and corrected himself. "No, I see it clearly now. It's not Buzz, but Burt." He opened his eyes and looked around, searching the crowd.

At first nothing happened. But then, someone in the last row, a skinny, slender man with dark sunglasses stood up and squealed in an excited voice, "Me… It's me. My name is Burt. Burt Jungles. I am blind since birth."

Sharlan Tan raised both of his hands and shouted out a word of praise. "Come forward, Burt."

The man, with the aid of a seeing-eye-dog stepped forward. One of Sharlan Tan's bullies jumped up and ran over to help Burt Jungles to climb up onto the stage. When he had positioned Burt right in front of the prophet, a warm smile appeared on Sharlan Tan's face. "Hello, Burt, your days of suffering are over."

Burt did not reply but stared through his sunglasses at the prophet.

"Are you from Calmhaven?" Sharlan Tan continued.

"No Sir," Burt replied. "I am from Boulder Valley. I heard about you, so someone brought me here."

"Praise god," Sharlan Tan gushed. "Today happiness has come to Boulder Valley, for the spirit expressly told me you will see today."

Without wasting another minute he placed his hands over Burt Jungle's eyes and shouted in the microphone, "Blindness, be gone. In the name of heaven."

Burt didn't move.

He stood transfixed.

Everyone in the tent grew still, all eyes were fixed on Sharlan Tan and Burt Jungles.

"Burt," Sharlan Tan cried out. "Take off your glasses."

Burt lowered his head and ever so slowly he took off his glasses.

"Burt... how many fingers do I hold out before you?" Sharlan Tan held two fingers in front of Burt's eyes, and moved them back and forth as if they were a pendulum on a clock.

"I-I..." Burt stammered as Sharlan Tan held the microphone before his mouth. "I see... I can see! I see two fingers."

"Two fingers it is," Sharlan Tan yelled jubilantly. "Burt, you can throw your glasses away."

Burt looked around, grabbed his head with both hands and stammered, "I can see... I can see."

The crowd was in awe.

"Prove your faith, Burt," Sharlan Tan urged him. "Prove your faith by stepping on your glasses."

For a moment Burt looked up into Sharlan Tan's face with questioning eyes.

"I rebuke these doubts," Sharlan Tan continued. "Break your glasses."

Burt let out a roar, threw his glasses on stage and

stepped on them so hard that even the people situated on the last row could hear the breaking of glass.

"Well done, well done," Sharlan Tan kept on shouting and raised both of his hands in the air again while shouting out more praises.

Digby leaned over to Molly Gertrude. "We can't let this go on, Miss Molly Gertrude," he mumbled. "What are we going to do?"

Molly Gertrude did not answer. She herself had just been asking God the same question.

You shall not have to fight in this battle. The words Papa Julian had received were so comforting, but when was God going to do something? Surely it was nearing the time.

"You see what can be accomplished with the power of faith," Sharlan Tan shouted in the microphone when all the excitement ebbed away somewhat. He turned to Burt and told him with a grand smile, "Thank you Burt. You may leave the stage now."

Burt climbed down without anybody else's help, and hugged his seeing-eye-dog. "I will not need you anymore, Bailey," he told his dog, who barked in happy agreement and he walked away rejoicing.

Sharlan Tan urged the public to be still again and he closed his eyes again. His hand went up as it had before. He seemed to be in communication again with higher entities. "Arthritis," he cried out. "Somebody here has arthritis… It's a man, and god is telling me he wants to heal him."

Several hands shot up.

"That's me, Brother Tan," one cried out.

"No, it's me," another yelled.

But Sharlan Tan kept his eyes closed in concentration. "His name…," he finally spoke, "… starts with an… H."

Hierro Glyphen who sat on a bench in front of Molly Gertrude, froze. He turned around and looked at Molly Gertrude. "That's me… I thought this whole thing was a hoax, but it's not. I am going to get healed…"

CHAPTER TWELVE

A larm flashed over Molly Gertrude's face. "No, Mr. Glyphen," she cried out, "it couldn't be you."

But Hierro Glyphen had already raised both of his arms in the air and shouted out. "Me, that's me. My name is Hierro."

Sharlan Tan did not look in Hierro Glyphen's direction, but kept on staring the other direction in search of the right person. Another pair of arms flew up near the entrance of the tent, and Sharlan Tan nodded in pleased satisfaction. "There is the man," he said and pointed in his direction. A short, stocky fellow (Molly Gertrude figured he was close to seventy) kept on waving his hands in the air, and shouted, "My name is Hanson. And I need healing from my arthritis."

Sharlan Tan wanted to say something in the microphone, but something stirred within Molly Gertrude's heart.

This is it, Molly Gertrude. Speak up. This is what you have been waiting for.

Molly Gertrude did not consider herself to be very spiritual, and she was not one to claim she often heard the voice of God, but on this occasion she was convinced God was telling her to take action.

She jumped up from the bench and yelled as loud as she could with her old voice, "Heal them both, Mr. Tan. Apply the heavenly power to both men."

Several voices in the audience grunted their approval. "Yeah, two for the price of one," someone cried out.

Sharlan Tan didn't like it.

His 'I am in control' look had gone out the door and for a short, desperate moment, he looked at his bullies for help, but they could not offer him any advice. He licked his lips and motioned everyone to be silent. "I've never had such a request, but we will ask the spirit." He raised his arms again towards the top of the tent and he closed his eyes once more, apparently seeking help from the invisible realm. At last he muttered, "Ah... I see it now. The last name of the man who is up for immediate healing starts with a... G... Yes, it's a definite G. His initials are HG."

"Yes," Hierro shouted it out. "I knew it! I knew it! That's me. My name is Hierro Glyphen. I will never again mock religion."

Now Sharlan Tan's face turned a dark red. Molly Gertrude couldn't believe her eyes.

But the man that was called Hansen did not budge. "No," he shouted just as loud as Hierro Glyphen, "it's me, not him. My initials are HG as well. My name is Hanson Gaffy. Surely, the spirit means me."

Molly Gertrude turned to Digby. "My voice can't reach that far, but yours can. Shout out in your booming voice that Sharlan Tan needs to heal them both. We will have the crowd on our side."

Digby grinned. Finally some action. This was going better than he had expected.

He cleared his throat, placed both of his hands around his mouth and shouted as loud as he could, "Sharlan Tan... heal both men."

"Yeah, heal them both," many other spectators began

to yell as well, and soon the whole crowd chanted in unison, "Heal them both. Heal them both."

Sharlan Tan was rubbing his forehead. Molly Gertrude was convinced she could see him sweating profusely.

"Heal them both. Heal them both." The sound of the spectators rolled like a wave through the circus tent.

"All right," Sharlan Tan shouted at last. "Both men come here."

Hierro Glyphen turned around, and stared at Molly Gertrude with a victorious face. "Wish me luck, Miss Grey." Then he made his way through the crowd and limped forward to the stage.

As soon as he was out of sight, someone pulled on Molly Gertrude's sleeve. She thought it was Dora and without turning she mumbled, "What is it, Dora?"

"I am not Dora," came the voice. "I am Emily."

Emily?

Molly Gertrude turned abruptly, and stared into the youthful eyes of Emily Bimbleton. "Emily, what are you doing here?"

"I saw you when you entered the tent. Just like you I guess, I wanted to see what the rave was all about." She paused for a moment. "But then I saw that man... and I wanted to tell you, so I pushed my way through the crowd."

"What man?"

"The one you were talking to."

"Hierro Glyphen?" Molly cocked her brow.

"I don't know his name," Emily whispered, "but he's the one."

Molly Gertrude narrowed her eyes. "What do you mean?"

"You asked me the other day at the police station if I recognized that homeless fellow as the one who broke into the church..."

"Go on."

"I told you I did not, but that man that is now going to the stage to get prayer... he's the one I saw that night. I recognize the way he is limping. Everything fits. I am absolutely certain that he is the man you are looking for."

* * *

179

Molly Gertrude gasped and stared with wide, round eyes into Emily's serious face. "You are sure?"

"Absolutely," Emily bobbed her head.

"Thank you, Emily," Molly Gertrude mumbled at last, and considered the implications. "I must say I already had my suspicions, but now I am beginning to see the whole picture."

"Just wanted to say it," Emily said. She gave Molly Gertrude a shy smile, turned around, and worked her way back to her own spot.

Molly Gertrude leaned over to Dora and Digby. "You hear that?" she mumbled. "Hierro Glyphen knows a lot more than he told us."

Hierro Glyphen was just about to climb up on the stage and was being helped by one of Sharlan Tan's helpers.

"Do you think he's working with Sharlan Tan?" Dora asked. "How could we have missed that?"

"I don't think he's necessarily working with Sharlan Tan," Molly Gertrude cautioned her. "I think he is having genuine problems with arthritis. I don't think he is faking it."

"But Emily pin-pointed him as the one who broke into the church." Digby tilted his head.

"I think, he's sincerely hoping for relief from his problems," Molly Gertrude observed. "We have a few questions for him, but we still have no proof that either Sharlan Tan or Hierro Glyphen actually stole the book."

Another squeal from the microphone broke through our friends' musings and they looked back up. Both Hierro Glypen and Hanson Gaffy stood on either side of Sharlan Tan, who had forced a smile on his face and tried to act relaxed and confident. But by the way he was shuffling his feet around, Molly Gertrude could tell the man was not in his element.

"This is going to be interesting," Molly Gertrude said. "Let's see how Sharlan Tan is going to solve this problem."

Another microphone squeal pierced through the tent. Sharlan Tan moved the mike around with an apologetic grin and said, "Well, well, well. Never a dull moment when you are living for the lord."

His statement was met with a few laughs, but most people did not react and stared at the prophet with questioning gazes. Sharlan Tan lifted his chin, closed his eyes and motioned for everyone to be quiet once more. Only the occasional shuffling of feet, and a few coughs could be heard.

"I sense...," he began, "...a spirit of unbelief." His voice was droopy and sad. "Oh, why can't people believe, when the table is spread before them and they are invited to freely eat and drink of the heavenly delicacies. And yet, there are those who are filled with doubt." He stopped speaking and seemed to concentrate as if a new idea hit him. He gave a short nod, opened his eyes again and turned to Hanson Gaffy while casting the man a warm smile. "And yet in this man, I perceive no guile. In this man there is still a spirit of faith." He proceeded to place his hands on Hanson Gaffy's head and shouted loud and commanding, "Arthritis... be gone."

Like the man who had been healed from blindness, Hanson, at first, did not react, but then he folded out his hands and looked at his fingers. He moved them one by one, and cast a surprised look in the direction of Sharlan Tan. "The pain is gone... It's really gone."

"You hear that, people," Sharlan Tan shouted while he addressed the crowd. "The pain is gone." He turned back to Hanson Gaffy. "Dance for me. Show me you can dance without pain."

"I sure can!" Hanson shouted with joy, and as he said it, he began to run around the stage while wildly swinging his arms around. "No more pain," he yelled at the top of his lungs. "No more pain."

The crowd cheered.

"Now heal the other one," Digby shouted out above the crowd. "Now pray for Mr. Glyphen."

Sharlan Tan cast him an angry stare, but turned to look at Calmhaven's nervous curator.

"Please, Mister Tan... I would like to walk without pain too." Hierro Glyphen looked up at Sharlan Tan with hope-filled eyes. His words were clearly heard by all through the microphone.

"Sharlan Tan shook his head, "As I said, I sense unbelief. Even the prophet Jesus could not do many works one time because of the unbelief in the hearts of the hearers."

"Pray for him." Digby shouted again, and within seconds the crowd began to chant again. "Pray for him. Pray for him."

Sharlan Tan rocked back and forth in his place, and was clearly at a loss for words.

"Pray for him. Pray for him."

At last, he nodded and said, "I'll do my best, but I doubt if this man will be healed." He placed his hands on Hierro Glyphen's shoulder and a guttural roar escaped from his throat. "Arthritis, be gone."

Hierro Glyphen pressed his eyes together, while his fists, in spite of the pain, curled up into little balls. His nose began to twitch violently and it seemed he was expecting some sort of lightning bolt to come from the heavens that would touch and heal him.

The crowd stopped chanting. All eyes were on the stage.

Sharlan Tan cleared his throat. "Open your hands," he commanded.

Hierro Glyphen opened them.

At least he tried, but he couldn't.

"They are stuck," he stammered, while fear flashed over his face. "That happens sometimes. My fingers often get stuck in one position and I can't get them back, but now it's worse than ever." He offered both of his fists to Sharlan Tan. "Help me, Sir... please, help me."

Sharlan Tan wrinkled his nose. "Unbelief," he yelled once more. "If you would have had faith, you would be dancing right now, as did Mr. Gaffy. But it's your own unbelief that blocks the road to healing."

"I want to have faith," Hierro Glyphen cried out. "I honestly want to."

"Then dance for me," Sharlan Tan ordered.

Poor Hierro Glyphen. He made a small jump, his fists still curled up in little balls, but his face contorted in pain. "I-I can't."

"Unbelief has captured another victim tonight," Sharlan Tan said with a sigh and drooping shoulders. "Just as I expected. I told you so."

But Digby had had more than enough. He could not stand another minute of this disheartening show of deception. "It's not true," he yelled as loud as he could. "The reason Hierro Glyphen isn't healed has nothing to do with his so-called unbelief. He is not healed, because you are no real faith-healer. You are a fraud and a charlatan. You can't really heal anybody. You are nothing but a child of hell."

For a moment nobody spoke.

Digby's words had the impact of an explosion and all eyes turned to Digby. But the silence did not last long. It was clear Digby had thrown the cat among the pigeons, and a shockwave of discontentment washed over the crowd.

Sharlan Tan's face turned red, and now his fists curled up into little balls too, although he still seemed to master them as he lifted one finger to heaven and yelled at the top of his lungs, "Heresy."

His stooges rose from their stools as well. Wolf accidentally knocked one stool over and it rolled off the stage where it came crashing down on a garbage can that was placed nearby.

Sharlan Tan pushed Hierro Glyphen aside and now pointed his angry, crooked finger in the direction of Digby. "You should be afraid to speak against the servant of God! The anger of God will be kindled against you." *

It was clear however that he had lost his control over the crowd.

The people grew restless and stared at each other in confusion. Some were shouting angry curses at Digby, but others weren't so sure and seemed torn between two opinions. Many recognized him, and knew him to be a faithful police officer who was known for his integrity. Would a man like Digby tell lies? That was unlikely.

Sharlan Tan cried out a command to his henchmen. Wolf immediately climbed off the stage and pushed his way towards Digby.

Digby saw him coming. He grabbed his badge and held it up high in the air for all to see. "I am a police officer. I am here to restore order. Nobody should be doing anything foolish."

Molly Gertrude searched for JJ Barnes. Where was he?

She spotted him, still near the front, but he seemed in shock.

But then, just before Wolf reached Digby, there was the loud and crackling voice of someone who spoke through a megaphone. "That man is right," the voice cried out. "Sharlan Tan is a liar."

Wolf stopped. All eyes went in the direction of the new voice, and the pandemonium stopped, at least for the moment.

There, positioned on top of a VW bus stood a young fellow, dressed in the familiar T-Shirt that glorified Tan. He was holding a megaphone in his hand and asked the crowd to stay calm.

Molly Gertrude, Dora and Digby recognized him instantly.

"Elvis," Dora said, and her face lit up.

"Elvis?" Digby frowned.

"I work for Sharlan Tan," Elvis cried out from his elevated position. He shouted it out, bold and unafraid, and his angry voice filled the tent. "And I can testify that what this police officer is saying is absolutely true. The people that are supposedly getting healed were never sick in the first place." Elvis waved one of his arms in the air, hoping to give his speech more impact. "How do I know this? Because I did it myself. I once was staged as a boy with serious back problems. Sharlan Tan paid me $100 for my deception. He told me I was to tell everyone I had been ill for years and that nothing had ever helped me. Then, on stage, he prayed for me and I was to jump up and claim I was healed. But it was all a lie."

Sharlan Tan was enraged.

His face was no longer red, but had turned a bright purple. "Lies, all lies, designed to harm the work of God."

"Your so-called miracles are false," a small man with a red nose shouted.

"You pay people money to act sick, and then you

deceive them with your so-called Isaiah-seeds," a woman with ripped jeans and frizzy hair cried out.

"But I still need help with my alcohol problem," the man with his whiskey bottle yelled, not satisfied that his chance of healing seemed to be going out the door.

"All lies. It's all lies," Sharlan Tan screamed. He pulled out a whistle from under his garment and blew on it. His stooges heard the desperate sound, and immediately turned around and fought their way back to the stage.

Things were heating up fast, and Molly Gertrude feared some folks were so enraged that they might even end up harming Sharlan Tan.

At that moment Digby's phone went off. "It's JJ Barnes," he said to Molly Gertrude. "He's calling all units. Immediate assistance required at Waterside Snomp."

Digby put down his phone and grinned. "God worked. Just as you thought He would."

At that instant JJ Barnes had spotted Digby and pushed his way through the angry crowd. "Digby," he shouted from a distance. "Am I glad to see you. More police will be coming, but arrest the whole bunch.

All of them, Sharlan Tan, Hierro Glyphen, Hanson, all of them."

Digby couldn't suppress a smile. "Duty is calling Miss Molly Gertrude and Dora. I have a job to take care of. I will see you later at the police station."

* Numbers 12:8-9

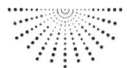

CHAPTER THIRTEEN

The atmosphere in the police station, the next day, was electrifying.

JJ Barnes was distraught, his face carried a scowl, and he resembled a football player that had been unceremoniously kicked out of the Super Bowl. His shoulders were drooping as he hung over his desk, and he kept softly moaning that he should have listened to Molly Gertrude earlier. "I really thought this man could help me with some of my problems," he muttered. "But I am going to get my $100 back. Imagine that... Isaiah-seeds. I must have been temporarily insane."

"Don't be too hard on yourself, Mr. Barnes," Molly Gertrude, who was sitting before his desk, tried to comfort him. "These conmen are professionals and are highly skilled."

He looked up at Molly Gertrude with glistening eyes. "You got him. You and Digby. And then to think that I am the one to protect the community from folks like this."

Molly Gertrude lightly stroked Barnes' forearm, something she had never done before, but she felt sorry for the husky police officer. "We all make mistakes. And...," she paused and lifted the index finger of her other hand, "... it's not too late to do something about it. The ball is in your court now, as we have everyone in custody at the station, so you are on the winning team."

That thought seemed to cheer JJ Barnes, and he cast Molly Gertrude a grateful smile. "Do you think we have enough proof against Sharlan Tan?"

Molly Gertrude nodded. "I would advise you to get a warrant, so you can search his motor home. I've got pictures on Digby's phone that are very incriminating."

JJ Barnes raised his bushy brows. "What kind of pictures? How did Digby get them?"

"Don't ask," Molly Gertrude stated. "Just go over to

his motor home and look for his notebook. But we have more. We have the testimony of Elvis, his employee."

JJ Barnes had heard enough. He pushed the button on his intercom and ordered his secretary to arrange a search warrant for Sharlan Tan's motor home.

When he was done he folded his hands and sighed. "And what about that book that you were asking me about. You told me you thought Sharlan Tan may have stolen that as well. Is it back already?"

"Not quite," Molly Gertrude said as she squeezed her chin. But then she added in confident tones, "But I think I know where it is, and what happened to it. Could we have everyone involved together, then we can solve this mystery as well."

"Who is everyone?"

"You of course," Molly replied, "and Digby, but especially the ones that have been arrested. Sharlan Tan, his helpers, and I understand you picked up Hierro Glyphen and Hanson Gaffy as well, so you can bring them too."

"All right," JJ Barnes mumbled. "I'll tell Digby to get everyone together this afternoon. I must say, I can't wait to hear what you have to say."

Sharlan Tan sat on a small stool, his legs spread out wide, and a dark scowl was covering his face. His hair was no longer in a tail, but was now hanging loosely over his shoulders. His face was scratched, and his priestly robe was badly ripped as he had struggled with Digby upon his arrest. "I will sue you all," he kept on hissing. "You are making a terrible mistake. You have no idea who you are messing with."

JJ Barnes shook his head. "I do," he said with a sneer. "You are the fellow that stole $100 from me."

Without caring for manners, Sharlan Tan spat on the floor. "It was a donation. Everyone knows that. You can't do anything about it, but if you release me, I may still forgive you."

At that instant, the door opened and Papa Julian and Bella entered.

As soon as Sharlan Tan recognized the pastor, his nostrils flared and he began to breathe more rapidly. "You," he fumed, "I *knew* you were behind all this." He lifted up his handcuffed hands, and pointed with one finger at Papa Julian. "Don't you know that he who touches the anointed, touches the apple of god's eye?"

"I've read that in the Bible," Papa Julian replied without showing any emotions. "I guess it depends on who is really the anointed of God."

Sharlan Tan was enraged and if it had not been for Digby, who stood right behind him, he may have jumped up in an effort to attack Papa Julian.

Then the others arrived.

First they led Hierro Glyphen in. The curator was limping as usual, and his nose twitched violently again. When he saw JJ Barnes, he began to moan, "It's all a mistake. I am not supposed to be here. I am a victim of Sharlan Tan's shenanigans."

"Quiet," JJ Barnes barked, and motioned for Digby to put the man on a stool as well.

Hanson Gaffy and Elvis were brought in, as well as Sharlan Tan's helpers. Wolf seemed especially distraught. Even Emily Bimbleton made her appearance.

Only Molly Gertrude and Dora were still missing, but just as JJ Barnes impatiently began to stare at the clock Molly Gertrude and Dora entered and found themselves a seat.

"Good," JJ Barnes licked his lips. "Let's start this meeting. Molly Gertrude?" he said, "The stage is all yours."

Molly Gertrude pressed her lips together, and for a moment she said nothing. At last she cleared her throat. "A book has been stolen from the church. A very valuable book."

"So?" Sharlan Tan hissed, "What does that have to with me?" And without waiting for Molly Gertrude's reply, he added, "And who are you anyway? The district superintendent or something like that?"

JJ Barnes wanted to bark his displeasure, but Molly Gertrude raised her hand and said, "Excuse me, Mister Tan. My name is Molly Gertrude Grey, and this is my helper, Dora Brightside. We run Calmhaven's marriage office."

Sharlan Tan's eyes narrowed into tiny slots and he backed away with a shudder. "I am not planning to get married any time soon, so what's the big deal."

"I am glad to hear that," Molly Gertrude answered. "I believe your prospects for marriage are rather slim, since I think you'll be going to prison."

Sharlan Tan veered up as if a snake had bitten him.

"Why? I am a victim of slander. I am a prophet of god."

"Quiet," JJ Barnes roared. "You owe me $100. Let Miss Grey speak."

Molly Gertrude studied Sharlan Tan's face for a moment and then said in quiet tones, "That's not true, Mr. Tan. You know very well why you are here, and you *did* know about the book in question."

Sharlan Tan shrugged his shoulders. "Can't remember. I've got more important things on my mind than books."

Molly Gertrude leaned her head forward. "I'll refresh your memory. You tried to coerce our pastor, Papa Julian, to give it to you, so you could sell it. We've got witnesses."

"Lies," Sharlan Tan fired back. "The man is just jealous. I even went to his house to make peace, but he and his wife threw me out. Nice witnesses they are." He averted Papa Julian and Bella's gaze, and then mumbled, "What book are we talking about anyway?"

"Pilgrim's Progress," Molly Gertrude explained. "An original edition, written by a man called John Bunyan."

Sharlan Tan seemed to want to change tactics. He forced a smile on his face, and switched to his kind, suave preacher's approach. "Ah… Pilgrim's Progress. An excellent book. I remember hearing about it. But I never stole such a book."

"But you knew about the book, because you asked Papa Julian to donate it to you, right? Who told you about the existence of that book?" Molly Gertrude continued.

"God told me," Sharlan Tan replied with the conviction of a math student, who has been asked how much two plus two equaled.

"Wrong answer," Molly Gertrude sneered. "I will tell you who told you about that book." She turned to Hierro Glyphen. "It was Mr. Hierro Glyphen, the one who refused to donate paintings to your good cause, and the one you in turn failed to heal from his arthritis."

Sharlan Tan glared at Hierro Glyphen, who shifted uneasily upon his stool. "I don't recall ever seeing that man."

"Is that so?" Molly Gertrude queried. She turned to the curator. "Is Mr. Tan speaking the truth, Mr. Glyphen?"

Glyphen lowered his gaze. "Well... eh...," he stammered, "Not quite. We did see each other. A little bit."

"When was that, Mr. Glyphen?"

The curator wiped his brow. "As you said, Mr. Tan came to ask me if I would be willing to donate paintings for the building of a new church. He told me God would bless me, and..." his voice trembled, "...he was quite pushy about it. But these paintings he was referring to are not mine to give away, and what is more, I could never willingly part with... with my..."

"Children?" Molly Gertrude asked. "Isn't that how you see all these old relics, as your children?"

Hierro Glyphen pressed his lips together and blushed. "You may say so, yes," his reply was barely audible.

"And how do you think Mr. Tan knew that Papa Julian had that valuable book in his possession?"

"I told him," Hierro Glyphen whispered.

Molly Gertrude cocked her brow. "Why did you do that?"

Hierro Glyphen looked down again. "It was a

mistake." He lifted his eyes and cast an angry look at Sharlan Tan. "He seemed so interested in old valuable artifacts, and I felt I had finally met somebody with the same passions. It got me excited and off guard. I had just heard about John Bunyan's book, and I was so excited about it."

Molly Gertrude rubbed her brow. "Where had you heard about John Bunyan's book?"

"In Miss Marmelotte's. I usually go there for lunch, and people were talking about it. I just overheard them."

Molly Gertrude leaned back. "People were talking about it openly in Miss Marmelotte's?" She turned around and stared at the others.

Papa Julian pulled on his brow and shook his head. "That was supposed to have been a secret, remember Miss Molly Gertrude? Did you tell anyone?"

Now it was Molly Gertrude's turn to blush. "Well, eh yes, I couldn't keep it a secret and Digby…"

Molly Gertrude narrowed her eyes. "Digby?"

Digby's ears got red. "Well, eh, I may have told a few

friends. I didn't see any harm in it, and it was an important book, wasn't it?"

Papa Julian glared at Sharlan Tan. "You told me you got a prophecy from God that I had that book, but it wasn't a prophecy at all."

"God works in mysterious ways," Sharlan Tan glared back. "But, I still didn't steal your book."

"There you are right," Molly Gertrude said. "You did not. You have an alibi for the night of the theft." She pointed to Elvis and the Sharlan Tan's henchmen. "There are several people that can verify that you went to sleep early the night of the break in. What's more, we have a witness who saw the robber breaking in the church, and he does not fit your profile."

Sharlan Tan smacked his lips in satisfaction. "Well, that settles it. Maybe you can relieve me from these cuffs as well."

"No, we can't and we won't," Molly Gertrude replied. "You are not here because I think you stole the book. You are here on much more serious charges, such as cheating and manipulating people in the name of God."

"You've got no proof," Sharlan Tan howled.

"We've got plenty of proof," Molly Gertrude answered in a calm manner. "Digby has just been searching your motor home, and he found some interesting stuff. What's more, we've got several witnesses. To be honest, I am not sure if the judge will act very favorable upon your antics. If you have any money stashed away somewhere, you may need it to get yourself a good lawyer."

For a moment, Sharlan Tan stared at Molly Gertrude with a stony face, but then, like the walls of Jericho after the Israelite army had walked around it seven times, it appeared Sharlan Tan's battlements began to crumble as well. His face became rather pale, and his breath became labored. "I-I can't get any air," he mumbled. "I feel sick."

"Bring him back to his cell, and call the doctor." JJ Barnes barked.

Digby jumped up, and while a young police officer ran out to notify the doctor, Digby dragged Sharlan Tan out of the room to bring him back to his cell.

"Well," JJ Barnes said with a frown when Digby had returned, "If Sharlan Tan didn't steal the book, then who did it?"

Molly Gertrude's face became sad and she turned to Hierro Glyphen. "It's your limp that gave you away,

Mr. Glyphen. The very limp you wanted to get healed from, betrayed you."

For a moment it was very still in the room, but then and without warning, Hierro Glyphen broke out sobbing. "It's true... I did it. I confess. I snuck into the church and it was me who took the book."

Molly Gertrude leaned forwards and placed her hand on the man's leg. "It was a very foolish thing to do, Mr. Glyphen, but I don't think you meant any harm. You wanted to guard that book from falling into the wrong hands."

"That's right," Hierro Glyphen sniffed. "When I first heard about the book, I wanted to go over to Papa Julian, just so I could study it. But then Sharlan Tan visited me. While he was very friendly at first, he became more and more pushy and unpleasant. When he left, I realized I had told him about the book, and I became scared he would break into the church and steal it." He wrung his hands in despair and tried to stop the twitch in his nose, but his emotions got the better of him, and his sniffing turned into sobbing.

"I did it to prevent evil people from stealing and selling it." Hierro Glyphen looked up at Molly

Gertrude with drooping eyes. "H-How did you find out?"

"Actually, I thought it was you the day we met in your office a few days ago." Molly Gertrude answered.

"You did? H-How did you figure that out?"

"I didn't have proof, Mr. Glyphen," Molly Gertrude said, "but there were several hints that pointed in your direction. The first one was the stained glass window that was taken out of the church. You would have never wanted to break such a beautiful, old window as was in Papa Julian's church. You even call old things your children, so you very carefully and with great skill removed the window so as to not damage it. Sharlan Tan, or a regular thief couldn't have cared less about a mere stain glass window."

Hierro Glyphen wiped a tear off his face and there was even a hint of a smile when he thought back of it. "I was very careful, wasn't I?"

"Is there more proof?" JJ Barnes bellowed.

"There is," Molly Gertrude continued. "Mr. Glyphen gave himself away when he told us the book had been hidden in a wooden box that was stored in the basement of the church. Papa Julian had not told anybody about that. Dora and I were the only ones who knew that because Papa Julian had told us, but nobody else knew. Only the thief would have known."

Hierro Glyphen looked miserable.

The blood had drained from his face and he was trembling all over. "W-Who is going to take care of Greenacre Museum if I am going to prison?" he mumbled while he stared at the ground.

"You should have thought of that, before you became a thief," JJ Barnes growled. "You will be charged to the full extent of the law."

For a moment it was still in the room, and it was Papa Julian who broke the silence. "No, Mr. Barnes, I press no charges."

Barnes looked up, a scowl on his face. "No charges? The man is a thief."

Papa Julian shrugged. "No charges, Mr. Barnes. Obviously, I can't condone anyone breaking into my church and stealing stuff, but I don't think Mr. Glyphen is a regular thief, and he should be treated with mercy. I feel it's what God wants me to do."

"Mercy?" JJ Barnes rubbed his brow. Then a smile broke out on his face and he nodded. "That's a mighty good thing to do, Papa Julian. But I hope we won't let Sharlan Tan off the hook? He still owes me $100."

"We won't," Molly Gertrude said. "That man has a lot more to answer for than just your $100."

"In that case," JJ Barnes said as he turned to Hierro Glyphen, "you are free to go."

Hierro Glyphen looked up, a look of relief flooding his face. "Really? I can go back to Greenacre Museum?"

Molly Gertrude's face held the hint of a frown. "It seems like that, Mr. Glyphen. But the first thing you should do is return the Pilgrim's Progress to Papa Julian."

"Of course," Hierro Glyphen said with a grand smile. "Right away."

"No need," Papa Julian spoke while he held up one of his hands. "I wish to donate the Pilgrim's Progress to the Greenacre Museum. Mr.Glyphen is right. Such a book should never be sold. It carries the spirit of the past, and it is a wonderful monument to the love of God. The Greenacre Museum is the only place where it truly belongs."

Hierro Glyphen's eyes widened. "I-I...," he

stammered, "This is better news than getting healed from my arthritis. And..." he added while he looked up into Papa Julian's face, "...maybe it's time I learn a bit more about the God Who is willing to show mercy to a man like me."

"That sounds like a wonderful idea." Papa Julian returned Hierro Glyphen's statement with a smile.

"Well," JJ Barnes said, "That just about wraps it up. Except..." he narrowed his eyes and stared at Sharlan Tan's helpers, including Elvis and Wolf, "... what are we to do with these fellows." He turned to Papa Julian. "Please don't give me the mercy-speech."

"Why not?" Papa Julian grinned. "Without Elvis' help, things would not have been so easy. Because of him, we got the big fish, so maybe we should leave it at that." Then he stared at Wolfgang Crossley. The man shuffled his feet around and did not dare look into Papa Julian's face. "And you, Wolf? What do you think about all this?"

Wolf shook his head and for a few seconds kept staring at the floor.

"Wolf?"

At last Wolfgang Crossley looked up. "I-I was a fool,

Papa Julian. I had no idea. I was blinded by my greed."

"Glad to hear you say that, Wolf," Papa Julian said. "Please know that Calmhaven's Trinity Church is always open to you."

"That's it?" JJ Barnes asked, while he wrinkled his nose.

"No," Papa Julian answered. "I'll say to these folks what Jesus said to the adulterous woman, "Go, and sin no more." *

*John 8:11

CHAPTER FOURTEEN

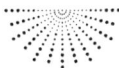

D ora was quite familiar with the road that lead to Boulder Valley. They were making good time, and that was important, as they had an appointment at ten sharp in Boulder Valley's Federal Prison. The motor of her Kia Rio was humming happily along as Dora steered the car over the winding road leading into Boulder Valley. Papa Julian was situated on the back seat, and Molly Gertrude sat in her usual seat right next to Dora.

They were on their way to see Sharlan Tan, but they had no idea what the man wanted.

He had written a short note to Papa Julian, requesting that the pastor come. Sharlan Tan had not given any details, except he had written that it was urgent.

"Urgent?" Papa Julian had wondered when he had read the note, sent to him in the special grey envelope from the Federal Prison. "What can be so urgent?"

The false prophet had been sentenced to two years in prison, and had only served six months so far.

"Don't know," Molly Gertrude had replied. "Will you go down there to find out?"

"How can I not go," Papa Julian had answered. "If a man is asking for me, I have little choice, do I?" But then he had asked if Molly Gertrude would be willing to come along.

Molly Gertrude had grinned. "How can I not go?" she had said. "If a man asks for my help, I have little choice."

Thus it happened that early that morning, after Bella had served them a hearty breakfast, they all climbed in and Dora had started the engine.

Traffic was heavy in Boulder Valley and the prison was situated all the way on the other side of the city.

"Will we make it on time?" Papa Julian mumbled

when they had to wait in a traffic jam. He was getting a little nervous.

Molly Gertrude chuckled. "I heard Sharlan Tan has another meeting at five past ten." She turned around and cast Papa Julian an encouraging smile. "Don't worry, Papa Julian. I don't think the man has a lot of appointments on his agenda today, so even if we are a bit late, it's not going to be a problem."

And Molly Gertrude was right.

When they finally arrived at the prison complex even though they were fifteen minutes late, they were ushered inside without any problems.

The grey concrete walls, all surrounded by razor wire, looked ominous and dark. What a lonely, dreadful and forlorn place it was. Molly Gertrude swallowed hard when she followed Papa Julian to the entrance and he pushed the button to announce their arrival. She was reminded of something she read once in a newspaper and that had made a deep impression upon her soul. "If you want total security, go to prison. There you're fed, clothed, given medical care and so on. The only thing lacking... is freedom." * It felt strangely true.

"Julian Maxwell?" the guard said while he checked his computer screen in the office near the entrance. "Yes, that is correct, you are expected." He glanced at Molly Gertrude. "I take it you must be his mother." He typed in something on his computer and then mumbled something about Dora being his wife, information that disappeared into the computer as well.

Dora wanted to object, but Molly Gertrude shook her head, and whispered, "Just let it be, for now."

"All right," The man looked up and pushed a button. An iron door in the hallway nearby opened up, and a guard stepped out. When he saw Molly Gertrude and Dora he winced. "Two women? I-I need to frisk you all."

Dora glared at him and waved her finger in front of his nose. "Don't you touch me."

The man hesitated, and walked over to a phone that was hanging nearby on the wall and took the receiver off the hook. He spoke a few words into the receiver and hung it back up. "We've got the kitchen lady coming. She can frisk you," he said with a scowl.

Dora was not pleased, but Molly Gertrude gave her a smile and said, "Come on, Dora, this is how life in prison goes. Just be happy you don't have to spend your days in here. This is the place where seconds gradually turn into hours, and hours into days, all without you making any progress."

Soon, the kitchen lady appeared. She was a curvy, buxom woman, and her arms could almost be compared to sturdy sledgehammers, but she was good at her job and minutes later they were led all three into the visiting area where they had to wait for Sharlan Tan.

There was nobody else in the room besides two serious looking guards. They were dressed in their prison uniforms, and were holding rifles. It was clear they were not visiting a member of the elite in the Hilton Hotel. They were in prison, the place designed to break obstinate human beings, something which was apparently only possible in drab, dreary surroundings. The windows were all barred, and the furniture which consisted of metal tables with adjoining, uncomfortable stools, were screwed down to the floor, so no inmate couldn't use it as a possible weapon.

Dora no longer had the courage to complain. The atmosphere was just too depressing. Papa Julian seemed to be in prayer.

And then, at last, another door opened and a guard

stepped in, followed by Sharlan Tan. The prophet no longer wore his priestly robe. They had now clothed him in the familiar orange prison garb. But there were no chains around his ankles and his hands.

Molly Gertrude figured that since he had not actually committed a crime as serious as a killing, he was on a less strict prison program. Still he did not look good at all.

As he approached, a shock went through Molly Gertrude's body.

He looked terrible. His deep-set eyes were surrounded by dark circles and his sunken cheeks, which had been fresh and rosy at the time when he had camped out in Calmhaven, had turned a ghostly grey.

When he saw Papa Julian, his sad, lost eyes lit up for a moment. He barely acknowledged Molly Gertrude and Dora and plopped himself down on one of the stools.

"Hello Sharlan," Papa Julian began. "You wanted to see me. How are you?"

Sharlan Tan stared at his hands that were resting before him on the metal table. Molly Gertrude could see he was fighting with his emotions and that he struggled for words. She would probably not be doing much better if she wore his shoes.

At last, Sharlan Tan licked his parched lips and whispered something so soft that not even Papa Julian could hear it.

"Excuse me?" the pastor leaned closer. "I did not hear you."

Sharlan Tan cleared his throat. This time his words came out louder, and they shocked his visitors.

"I am dying."

Molly Gertrude sat straight up. Papa Julian blinked his eyes and leaned forward.

"What do you mean?" the pastor said. "You are only about thirty-some years. You will be out of this mess before you know it, and then you can still make something out of your life."

Sharlan Tan shook his head. "No Papa Julian... I am *really* dying. The doctor said so."

"The doctor?" Papa Julian narrowed his eyes. "What's wrong with you?"

Sharlan Tan shrugged his shoulders. "Some bug. I don't know. My liver is infected and it's spreading everywhere."

"H-How long do you still have to live?"

Sharlan Tan looked up. There was nothing left of his former strong, chiseled features, and his supposedly charming, hypnotic eyes had lost all of their fire. "Weeks, maybe a month… I don't know."

"I am so sorry to hear, Sharlan," Papa Julian whispered. "Death comes to us all, but the passing can be a scary moment. Are you prepared?"

"That's precisely it," Sharlan Tan replied. "I am afraid to die." He paused for a moment, trying to collect his thoughts. "When I first came here and I lost my freedom, I was enraged. I am not proud to say it, but I cursed you and all the people in Calmhaven… but I have had a lot of time to think as well. And then came that dreadful day when I was diagnosed with my sickness, and the doctor told me I was dying… well I began to see everything in a whole new light."

"What light is that?" Papa Julian asked.

Sharlan's eyes began to glisten. "There's no hope for me. I wish I could undo some of the terrible stuff I've done, but I can't turn back the clock. There is nothing to look forward to, but a fearful, black, fuming sea of darkness, and I am afraid of it. I mean,

I have been so wicked and bad. I don't think the afterlife will look very kindly on the likes of me."

And there, to Molly Gertrude's amazement, a tear rolled out of the eyes of the man who had claimed to be such a mighty prophet, but who had been nothing but a fraud. The tear splattered onto the metal table before him.

Papa Julian placed his hand on Sharlan's arm. "Take Jesus, Sharlan. Just take Jesus. Just tell Him you are so very sorry for the lies you have preached. He'll understand."

"He can't," Sharlan sobbed. "He won't. I have deceived so many people, and all in His name. It says in the Bible that it would be better to be thrown into the sea with a millstone tied around my neck than to have caused one of these little ones to stumble. * I have cause many little ones to stumble."

Molly Gertrude could see that Papa Julian was deeply troubled. Papa Julian had such a soft heart and she knew the man was desperately trying to reach out to the man who had literally cursed him and tried to undermine his ministry.

"You can't be too bad for Jesus, only too good," Papa Julian said. "He's the real miracle worker. He performed the real miracles. He turned water into wine, he truly healed the sick, calmed the storm, walked on water, and He even raised the dead. But the most important of them all, He conquered death itself, and brought hope and salvation! Through Him we can have eternal life without sorrow, worries and fear."

Sharlan Tan shook his head. "Too late, pastor... it's too late. But I asked you to come because I needed to tell someone that I am sorry. Thank you that you at least came and gave me that chance." He forced a small smile through his tears and said, "Frankly, I thought you would not want to come. I wouldn't have wanted to come and see someone like me."

"Just take Jesus, Sharlan. He truly cares."

But the man shook his head. "I can't face Him, pastor. I just can't. But you can do me one favor. Will you pray for me? I do not think God will hear my prayers, but surely, He will hear yours."

Papa Julian stared at the man and pressed his lips firmly together. Molly Gertrude could sense her pastor's desire to take Sharlan Tan by the hand and gently lead him further. But the man himself had to take the last step. Here was a man who knowingly led countless people astray in the hopes of filling his own pockets, who was getting his just reward, and who knew the end of the road was approaching. Here was a man who could not count on the mercy of the world, but was still welcome in the Kingdom of God, if he would only be willing to forsake his pride and his fears, and would throw himself fully on the mercy of the one he had so blatantly misrepresented.

At last Papa Julian gave Sharlan a nod. "Of course I will pray for you." He turned to Molly Gertrude and Dora. "Will you join me in prayer?"

As Molly Gertrude stared at the miserable heap of humanity before her, who, with trembling hands had asked for prayer, she could feel the last bit of anger and resentment she still felt towards this man ebb away. Clearly the Spirit was yearning for the heart of this miserable man. "I would be honored, Pastor," she simply said.

And so it happened that they all four bowed their heads and Papa Julian poured out his heart before the throne of God on behalf of Sharlan Tan.

One hour later, they were outside of the prison again and Dora started the Kia Rio in order to drive them back to Calmhaven.

For the longest time no one said a thing. The spirit was just too strong.

When they arrived in Calmhaven and Molly Gertrude offered them a hot cup of tea, both Dora and Papa Julian declined. And when Dora didn't even want to stay for a Citrus Lemon Curd cookie, Molly Gertrude knew it had been an extraordinary visit.

* Eisenhower

** Luke 17:2 NIV

* * *

Two weeks later, early in the afternoon the bell rang at Molly Gertrude's house.

It was a long ring, and then it rang again. It was urgent. Molly Gertrude had just started a new detective novel and she frowned. *What now?*

She forced herself up out of the chair, and when she opened the door she stared at the panting figure of Papa Julian. The man had been running. Sweat glistened on his brow, and he was out of breath.

For a moment, Molly Gertrude feared he was bringing bad news, but then she noticed, in spite of his heavy breathing, that his eyes were shining and there was a smile on his face.

"What is it, Pastor? What in the world got you so excited?"

Without saying a word, Papa Julian handed her a letter he had been carrying, and he leaned against the wall to catch his breath.

Molly Gertrude raised her brow and stared at it.

It was a grey envelope. The kind they used in the Federal Prison.

"Is it about Sharlan Tan?" she asked Papa Julian while she pulled the letter out. "D-Did he die?"

"Just read it," Papa Julian replied.

Thus, while Papa Julian studied her, she began to read, and as she did, excitement rose in her heart as well. It was not about Sharlan Tan's death at all, but it was written by the man himself in clear, bright handwriting.

Boulder Valley

Federal Prison

September

· · ·

Dear Papa Julian

I was raised by my God-fearing parents. They taught me the Scriptures. I sang them, I memorized them, and I could dream them. And yet, I never knew the true God behind it all. God was as distant to me as the stars in the heavens. Thus it was easy for me to use God for my own profit. After all, who cares about a star that is a million miles away from us.

And then I came to Calmhaven.

It became my spiritual Waterloo, from where I was sentenced to Boulder Valley Federal Prison; the end of the road for a wretch like me.

Then you, Molly Gertrude and Dora Brightside prayed for me...

There are no words to describe what happened. While I deceived countless innocent people with my so-called healings and miracles, God performed a miracle of His own upon me, the most wretched person of all.

After your prayer that day a few weeks back, I felt light.

That night, for the first time in months, I fell asleep without fear. And then, when I awoke the next morning I felt strangely happy. It was almost as if new energy coursed through my body, and I asked to see the doctor.

I will spare you the details, but my sickness is gone.

The doctors cannot even find a trace of my illness. I am completely healed. Me, the fake healer, found healing at the hands of a merciful God.

Molly Gertrude stopped reading, as tears welled up in her eyes and she could no longer see the words. She dropped her hands and stared into the eyes of her faithful pastor friend. "How great is our God, Papa Julian... How infinitely wonderful and great...

Thank you so much for reading, *The Dead Man's Stolen Book*. We hope you really enjoyed the story. If so, leaving a review is a great way to let others know (reviews are such a great encouragement to our authors also!). Leave a Review Now!

Also, make sure to sign up to receive PureRead Donna Doyle updates at PureRead.com for more great mysteries, exclusive offers and news of our new releases. We love to surprise our readers and would love to have you as part of our reader family!

Much love, and thanks again,

Your Friends at PureRead

* * *

MORE MOLLY GREY MYSTERIES...

Wedding Cake Wipeout

The Bridal Dress Disaster

A Fishy Murder So Foul

The Mystery of the Missing Bride

Missing Cash & The Corpse in a Cabin

BOXSET READING ENJOYMENT

ENJOY HOURS OF CLEAN READING WITH SOME OF OUR BESTSELLING BOXSETS...

Here at PureRead we love to offer great stories and great value to our readers.We have a growing library of amazing clean read boxsets that deliver dozens of delightful stories in every bundle. Here are just a few, or browse them all and grab a bargain on our website...

Look for PureRead titles on Amazon or visit our website at
PureRead.com/boxsets

PureRead CHERISHED 42 Book Clean & Wholesome Story Box Set

PureRead Clean Reads Box Set Volume II

PureRead Clean Reads Box Set Volume I

PureRead Christmas Stocking of Stories

PureRead Terri Grace Legacy Boxset

Seasons of Regency Romance Boxset

Rainbow Mountain Brides Boxset

Mega Amish Romance Boxset

Christian Love 21 Book Contemporary Romance Boxset

** BROWSE ALL OF OUR BOX SETS **

http://PureRead.com/boxsets

ABOUT PUREREAD

T hank you for reading!

Here at PureRead we aim to serve you, our dear reader, with good, clean Christian stories. You can be assured that any PureRead book you pick up will not only be hugely enjoyable, but free of any objectionable content.

We are deeply thankful to you for choosing our books. Your support means that we can continue to provide stories just like the one you have just read.

PLEASE LEAVE A REVIEW

Please do consider leaving a review for this book on Amazon - something as simple as that can help others just like you discover and enjoy the books we publish, and your reviews are a constant encouragement to our hard working writers.

LIKE OUR PUREREAD FACEBOOK PAGE

Love Facebook? We do too and PureRead has a very special Facebook page where we keep in touch with readers.

To like and follow PureRead on Facebook go to **Facebook.com/pureread**

OUR WEBSITE

To browse all of our PureRead books visit our website at PureRead.com

Printed in Great Britain
by Amazon

39795406R10138